Olivia Bean, Trivia Queen

ALSO BY DONNA GEPHART

As If Being 12¾ Isn't Bad Enough,
My Mother Is Running for President!

How to Survive Middle School

Olivia Bean, Trivia Queen

a novel by
DONNA GEPHART

DELACORTE PRESS

Text copyright © 2012 by Donna Gephart
Jacket art copyright © 2012 by Angela Martini

All rights reserved. Published in the United States by Delacorte Press, an imprint of Random House Children's Books, a division of Random House, Inc., New York.

Delacorte Press is a registered trademark and the colophon is a trademark of Random House, Inc.

Visit us on the Web! randomhouse.com/kids

Educators and librarians, for a variety of teaching tools, visit us at randomhouse.com/teachers

Library of Congress Cataloging-in-Publication Data
Gephart, Donna.
Olivia Bean, trivia queen / Donna Gephart. —1st ed.
p. cm.
Summary: After overcoming a number of obstacles, especially in the subject of geography, Olivia is on her way to Hollywood to appear on *Jeopardy!* and, she hopes, to reunite with her father who left the family two years ago.
ISBN 978-0-385-74052-4 (hc) — ISBN 978-0-375-98952-0 (lib. bdg.) — ISBN 978-0-375-89940-9 (ebook)
[1. Curiosities and wonders—Fiction. 2. Jeopardy! (Television program)—Fiction. 3. Fathers—Fiction. 4. Divorce—Fiction.] I. Title.
PZ7.G293463Oli 2012
[Fic]—dc22
2011006023

The text of this book is set in 13-point Goudy Old Style.
Book design by Stephanie Moss

Printed in the United States of America
10 9 8 7 6 5 4 3 2 1

First Edition

"It's fun to be smart, Livi!" —Charlie Bean

If only . . .

Jeopardy! Round

Who Is Not My Dad?

It's 7:26 p.m., and you know what that means.

Little Bother is upstairs in his room, ramming Matchbox cars into the furniture, each other and probably DJ, our orange tabby. Mom's in the kitchen, washing dinner dishes. Neil's in there, too, drying dishes. And singing.

Conditions would be perfect for me to enjoy a quiet game of *Jeopardy!* in the living room by myself, except for Neil's singing. It's not like he's crooning softly, either, and being considerate of other people in the house. Neil's belting out an Aretha Franklin song like he's auditioning for *American Idol.* And he's completely mangling the lyrics.

"What it is you want," Neil practically shouts. *"Baby, I got it."*

Mom's laughter rings out over the sound of running water.

If it's possible, Neil seems to be ramping the volume up even more. *"All I'm askin' of you, my lady,"* he sings/shouts, *"is just little bits of respect when you come home."*

Mom chimes in, *"Just little bits."*

I can't help but smile at the happiness in Mom's voice.

"Hey, my lady." Neil's voice ruins my mood.

"Just little bits," Mom sings.

"Whenever you get—"

"Stop!" I scream. *"Jeopardy!* is almost on!"

Mom skids out of the kitchen into the dining room, a dish towel draped over her shoulder and a soup ladle clutched in her left hand—the hand that used to hold her wedding ring. She grins at me like this is a big joke and sings into the ladle as though it were a microphone. *"Just little bits."*

Neil stands behind her and puts his hands on her hips. *"My lady!"* he sings into Mom's hair.

She looks up at him and smiles. *"Little bits."*

They sway back and forth.

Yuck. "Um," I say. *"Jeopardy!* is about to start. Could you *please* take your little show on the road?" What I don't say is: *Our house used to be nice and quiet before Neil moved in one month, three weeks and five days ago.* Not that I'm counting or anything.

"*Jeopardy!*," Neil says, and looks at Mom.

She nods toward the living room. Toward me!

My shoulders slump. I like it better when Neil has to work at the library until they close at nine. On those nights, it's just me, Mom and Charlie for dinner—just like it was before he moved in. And I get to watch *Jeopardy!* alone.

As Neil heads my way, Mom snaps him on the butt with the kitchen towel. *Thwack!*

He leaps forward.

"Adorable," I mutter. "Barfingly adorable."

I strain to remember whether Mom and Dad ever acted that way when they were together. Maybe in the beginning when they first met, but not any time I was around to see it. The only kind of music I remember Mom and Dad making together was loud fighting.

Just then, I hear the *Jeopardy!* theme music, so I push Mom and Dad out of my mind and focus on the TV.

"Mind if I join you?" Neil asks, pulling up a stool and sitting beside me without waiting for my answer. He leans forward and scratches his scruffy beard, which makes him look like a college professor . . . or a homeless person.

I'm silent, hoping he'll take the hint and go back into the kitchen with Mom. I want to say that there must be dishes that need drying, but I don't. I want to say that maybe this time, they can sing "Over the Mountains and Far Away," but I don't do that either.

Dad used to request that song when I learned to play violin in fourth grade. "Jelly Bean," he would say. "Could you please play 'Over the Mountains and Far Away'?" It took a bit of research to learn that Dad was teasing about my screechy playing. There is no song called "Over the Mountains and Far Away"; it was Dad's fun way of asking me to practice somewhere else.

Neil leans forward and rubs his hands together. "Ready, Olivia?"

I slide away from him, like we're repelling ends of magnets, and I don't answer.

Neil sighs, but stays where he is.

Maybe that should make me feel guilty, but I can't worry about hurting Neil's feelings right now. It's especially important that I focus on Jeopardy! tonight. The practice might help with tomorrow's geography test.

When I was younger and told Dad how much I wanted to be on Jeopardy!, he shook his head and said, "Oh, Olivia, you wouldn't do well on that show. There are a ton of geography questions, and geography just isn't your thing." Dad was right, of course. I am lousy at geography—it's my weakest subject—but I hope that if I study hard and get better at it, I can be on the show someday.

If I watch Jeopardy! now and hit the books later

tonight, maybe I won't completely bomb the test tomorrow.

As Alex Trebek introduces the three contestants—Jenny from Oklahoma, Jack from Nevada and Asia from Michigan—Charlie, aka Little Bother, rockets down the steps, a Matchbox car in each hand. He stops in front of the TV. "Bet you didn't know flamingos pee on their legs *on purpose* to cool off."

"Ew," I say. "And get out."

Charlie doesn't move.

Neil glares at him. "Charlie Bean, we've talked about this. *Jeopardy!* is on and it's Olivia's special thing. You need to go somewhere else." He leans close to Charlie's ear and whispers loudly, "I have it on good authority your mom's in the kitchen making brownies." When Charlie doesn't scoot, Neil adds, "With chocolate chips."

Charlie tilts his head like he's thinking about which would be more fun, eating brownies with chocolate chips or bothering me; then he zooms into the kitchen like a race car. I hear him tell Mom the flamingo fact.

It's no surprise that Charlie got the Bean gene for collecting trivia, but unlike me and Dad, Charlie loves gross trivia. Yesterday, he shared with us that an emetomaniac is a person who always feels like throwing up.

I'm pretty sure that little gem of information will *not* help me on tomorrow's geography test. I just hope I don't get so nervous when Ms. Lucas hands out the test papers that I become an emetomaniac in front of the whole class. Right now, though, I'm grateful Charlie's in the kitchen.

I can focus on *Jeopardy!*

Neil hunches forward, his bushy eyebrows furrowed.

Dad used to sit back while watching *Jeopardy!*, relaxed as Sunday morning. He'd answer about 90 percent of the questions, then wave his hand dismissively. "I should be on that show," he'd say. "I could do better than those bozos. It's easy."

Jeopardy! is not easy; Dad's just really smart and can hold a lot of information in his head, like when he plays blackjack and can remember which cards have already been played. I'm a lot like Dad when it comes to remembering information . . . except most geography facts.

Alex Trebek reads each category—"Elementary!, Quick Foods, Chairman of the Board, Famous Captains and 'CAT'-astrophes."

A tingly shiver runs through my body.

The game is about to begin.

Who Is the Boy with Two First Names?

Once the game begins, Alex Trebek moves things along fast, like he's a seasoned conductor leading his orchestra through three quick movements. He *is* seasoned; he's hosted more than four thousand games. And he's been hosting *Jeopardy!* since September 10, 1984. That's way longer than I've been alive!

"Elementary! for two hundred," the first contestant says.

Alex Trebek reads from a card. "This is the second element in the periodic table."

"What is helium?" Neil shouts at the same time as the contestant, but before I have a chance to open my mouth. And I knew the answer!

"Elementary! again for four hundred, please."

Alex Trebek says, "Oxygen was discovered by this man."

"Who is Joseph Priestley?" Neil says, the tendons in his neck tight.

I shake my head. I've got to pay more attention in science class. I can't let Neil beat me.

"Quick Foods for eight hundred."

It seems like Alex Trebek looks right at me and says, "Morgan Spurlock's 2004 fast-food documentary."

"What is *Super Size Me*?" I say, giving myself a mental pat on the back.

Neil puts up a hand for me to high-five him.

I turn toward the TV and pretend I don't see his hand. There will be no good sportsmanship when it comes to *Jeopardy!* Not today; not ever. Like my dad always says, if you're going to play, play to win.

Sometimes when I think about Dad and how much I miss him, I get a cramp in my stomach. I'm bent forward when the middle contestant chooses the next category.

"Chairman of the Board for four hundred."

"On a Scrabble board," Alex Trebek says, "the triple-word-score squares are this color."

I remember Mom and Dad playing Scrabble on the dining room table.

"Red!" Neil says, forgetting the question rule.

"What is red?" I say, pointing out Neil's mistake.

"Oh," he says. "You got me on that one." Then Neil looks at me and gently touches my shoulder. "Olivia, you look a little uncomfortable. You okay?"

I realize I'm still bent over and pull myself up, but my stomach still hurts. I want to jerk away from him, but I just nod. He must see the pain on my face, though, because he looks concerned.

"Want me to get your mom?"

I shake my head and focus on the TV. *I just want you to go away.* My stomach really does hurt, though, and not only because I'm thinking about Dad. I also can't stop worrying about tomorrow's test. I should probably go upstairs and study because there aren't many geography categories tonight, but I never miss *Jeopardy!*

Neil gets the next three answers right, which makes the back of my neck feel hot. We're both clueless about the fourth. And before we know it, it's time for the Double Jeopardy! round.

By the end of the game at eight o'clock, Neil has kicked my trivia-loving butt by correctly answering way more questions, including Final Jeopardy!: "Mount Everest is on the border of Tibet and this country." The correct question was "What is Nepal?" Dad would have gotten it, too, I bet. But I had no clue.

Which only makes me more worried about tomorrow's geography test.

"Good game," Neil says, and offers his hand for me to shake. Hair sprouts from his knuckles. He looks like a Chia Pet gone awry.

I take a deep breath and shake his hand limply, but don't say "Good game" back to him. But I also don't say, "Maybe you should shave your knuckles, Monkey Man," so I still feel like I'm being nice.

"Who won?" Mom asks, standing at the edge of the living room.

Pointing at himself with his hairy-knuckled thumbs, Neil says, "The winner and new world champ." He nods and pretends to grab imaginary lapels. "I guess it's safe to say I'm a legend in my own time."

Mom plants her hands on her hips. "You mean a legend in your own mind."

"Yeah," I mutter, hoping only Neil hears.

"Olivia," Mom says. "I'm assuming you gave Neil a run for his money. I don't want his head to swell so much he can't walk through the kitchen doorway and help me get those brownies out of the oven."

I take a whiff of the sweet, chocolaty aroma and my mouth waters. "I could have done better," I say, holding my stomach. "I was a little off tonight."

Mom slings an arm around my shoulders and

14

squeezes. "Worried about tomorrow's test? You've been studying, right?"

I nod, even though all I did today was stare at my globe—eyes glazed—for about twenty minutes before dinner. I was probably gazing right at Mount Everest, but nothing about it actually registered. My brain's like that when it comes to geography facts.

"Great," Mom says. "Then you're ready to be crowned Olivia Bean, Geography Queen."

"Hardly!" I practically shriek, and press a fist into my stomach. "No matter what I do, I can't remember all the rivers and cities. When it comes to geography, my brain is Teflon-coated. Nothing sticks."

"Oh, you'll do fine," Neil says.

I look right at him. "No, I won't. Dad says it's my worst subject."

"But you're so smart."

"At trivia," I point out. "I'm not good at the important things that would help me in school, like geography."

Mom gives my shoulders another squeeze and tilts her head toward Neil, which probably means *Forgive my daughter's rudeness*. Mom makes that gesture a lot. "Besides," Mom says. "You have something most kids don't."

In my mind, I run through the list of things I have that most kids don't. *What is a father who lives three thousand miles away? What is no best friend? Who is my mom's* really annoying live-in boyfriend? *What is a little bother who puts his racing cars into my cereal bowl? What is*—

"You have this," Mom says, and kisses the top of my head.

"Hair?" I ask. "You think the other kids in my class are bald?"

Neil laughs.

Mom glares at me. "Livi, you know what I mean. You have a big, beautiful brain."

The human brain weighs three pounds, I think, *and is 75 percent water.* "Mom, all those kids have brains, too." I feel stupid saying it. "Big, beautiful brains. But some of those brains can actually hold facts about landmasses and state capitals, unlike your daughter's."

"Says you," Mom says.

Says Dad, I think, but don't say it out loud.

My stomach really hurts.

Charlie races into the living room and skids to a stop in front of Neil. "Brownies!" He flaps his hands like a fish flopping on a hook. "Burning! Brownies burning!"

We all sniff at the same time.

"Right you are, little man." Neil rockets up and crosses the dining room in three long strides.

As I hear the oven door squeak open, Mom says, "Your brain is special, Olivia. It seeks out and absorbs trivia like a . . . sponge."

While most sponges live for only a few years, some species can live for more than two hundred years.

Maybe Mom's right.

"Livi, when it comes to learning and remembering facts, it's like you've been training for it your whole life."

I like the way that sounds, that I've been training for it my whole life. But that's not right—not when it comes to geography, anyway. Now, if it were a *Jeopardy!* competition, then I could say I've been training for it my whole life. And mean it.

Thinking about training reminds me of the time Nikki and I decided to train for the Disney Marathon. Of course, we'd never even run half a mile before, except in PE class, and then only when forced to by our evil teacher, Mr. Piltz. And Disney World is a thousand miles away, but Nikki had read about the marathon in a magazine and thought it would be fun to run through the theme parks together. We decided the best way to train would be to run ten miles a day every other day until we could build up to really long runs. The first day, we managed to jog about a quarter mile away from home and a quarter mile back before collapsing in a heap on our living room couch.

Mom was there with lemonade, Pop-Tarts and encouragement.

Nikki and I never did get back to running. And

now, with three thousand miles and a mound of bad feelings separating us, we'll never accomplish that goal together.

"Your mom's right," Neil says, walking in with the pan of brownies, spoons and napkins.

Charlie follows, stuffing a wad of brownie into his mouth. "Yeah, your mom's right," Charlie says, a shower of crumbs exploding. "Oooh, hot." He waves his hand in front of his lips and hops from foot to foot, as though that will help cool the brownie scorching his mouth.

"Lovely." Mom turns her back to Charlie and spoons out some brownie. She blows on it without taking a bite. "Olivia, one of the first books you ever read, when you were only four, was the encyclopedia."

I take a spoonful of warm brownie and smile at the memory of those big, moldy-smelling books from Mom and Dad's shelf in their bedroom. I loved looking at the pictures, and the way the entries were arranged from "A" to "Z." Those books had what seemed like an endless supply of facts about everything from aardvarks to zydeco music.

"When you were Charlie's age," Mom continues, "you used to beat your grandfather at *Jeopardy!* all the time."

"Of course I did," I say, biting into my scorched brownie. "Grandpa Jack had Alzheimer's."

"Not back then," Mom says.

I tilt my head.

"Not that bad, at least," she says, popping a loose chocolate chip into her mouth.

"Oh, no!" Charlie screams, reaching between his shoulder blades as though he forgot something that was supposed to be there. He runs back into the kitchen.

Neil shakes his head at Charlie and sits on the stool again. "Olivia, what's the one thing you're most worried about?"

Taking tests. Geography. Taking geography tests. But the thing I'm most worried about is . . . I look right at Neil and tell him the truth. "Tucker Thomas."

Mom laughs and a brownie crumb goes flying. "Tucker Thomas? Didn't your father call him the Boy with Two First Names?"

I smile, but remembering Dad makes my stomach hurt again. Dad always came up with funny names for everyone. Charlie is Tigger—the happy, bouncing character from *Winnie-the-Pooh*. Dad used to call Mom Marion the Librarian, which is kind of weird because even though her name is Marion, she's a newspaper reporter, not a librarian. And oddly enough, her boyfriend, Neil, actually is a librarian. I wonder what Dad would call him. Jerkface Who's Living in My House with My Kids? That one's a little long, I suppose.

I don't actually know how Dad feels about Neil. When we talk on the phone, he doesn't say much more than "How's Neil doing?" I assume he doesn't like Neil, but I really don't know. All I know is that *I* don't like having Neil here all the time. It wasn't as bad when he just visited sometimes, but now he actually lives here. He walks around in his bathrobe in the morning, with a forest full of chest hair showing. He sits at Dad's old place at the table when we eat. And he takes the newspaper into the bathroom, and when he emerges half an hour later, I need a gas mask to go in.

I miss having Dad here, even though the reason he left us is pretty awful. I can't think about that right now, though, because it will make my stomach hurt more.

Instead, I try to remember something nice about Dad. He made up five different nicknames for me—Butter Bean, Jelly Bean, String Bean, Beany Baby and Lovely Livi, which makes me melt when Dad says it, even though with eyeglasses, occasional zits and flat-as-a-flapjack hair, I'm anything but!

"What about Tucker Thomas?" Neil asks.

I shrug. "He's good at geography."

Mom says, "So?"

"So," I say. "He's really good at geography and loves to rub it in when he gets a better grade on a test than I do."

"Livi," Mom says. "I'm sure it's only good-natured teasing. You guys have been friends forever."

"Well, we aren't friends now. And Tucker Thomas's teasing is anything but good-natured!"

"Oh," Neil says, nodding, as though he understands some great truth about the universe.

He doesn't. Just because he's a librarian and is surrounded by books doesn't mean he understands a single thing about me. At least Dad knows I'm a geography ditz. He was the one who pointed it out to me in the first place. And Dad would never have trouble understanding why I'm nervous the day before a geography test.

Charlie dashes in, a dish towel tucked into the back of his pajama top like a cape. He skids to a stop and puffs out his chest. "Did you know there are 516,000 bacteria in each square inch of armpit?" He demonstrates this by lifting his right elbow, like a chicken's wing, and pointing to his pit.

"Fascinating," Mom says. "Disgusting, but fascinating."

"It's true," Charlie says. "I read it in Livi's Ripley's Believe It or Not! book in the kitchen."

Like me, Charlie started reading when he was four. Now he's a pretty good reader for a kindergartner.

Neil tousles Charlie's hair. "Way to be a guy, little man. Gross facts are cool."

Charlie grins like he just won a trophy or something, then slaps Neil five so hard that I'm sure Tucker Thomas and his parents must have heard it through the living room wall that separates our town houses.

Neil shakes out his hand, pretending Charlie's slap might have broken a couple of the twenty-seven bones in it.

Charlie raises his small fist and declares, "I'm Armpit Bacteria Man!" Then he darts up the stairs, stumbling midway, but he catches himself and keeps going.

I shake my head, amazed that Charlie doesn't get upset when he stumbles like that. He never gets frazzled or embarrassed, even when he does something really stupid, like wearing his bumblebee Halloween costume to school the day *before* his class party.

I wish I could be more like Charlie.

That way, I could go to school tomorrow without worrying about the geography test. I mean, if I can't ace a simple geography test, how will I ever get on *Jeopardy!*? And I *have* to get on *Jeopardy!*

To make matters worse, Tucker Thomas sits next to me. So when the test papers come back in a couple days, he'll see how badly I did and be sure to wave his perfect test score in my face.

Maybe if I went to school dressed as a bumblebee, no one would notice when I bomb the test. Or perhaps

I should stroll into class dressed as Armpit Bacteria Man. But I'm not going to do those things. I'm going to go to school dressed as me—Olivia Bean—and I'm pretty sure I'm going to fail that test.

Oh, my stomach is killing me.

What Is the Name of the Fifth Ocean?

After breakfast, I take one more look at my globe and give it a mighty spin for luck, but that doesn't quell the nervous feeling in my stomach. I grab my backpack and leave for school, thinking I might as well get this over with.

As I lock our front door, I recite the seven continents—"North America, South America, Europe, Australia, Africa, Asia and Antarctica." I'm so absorbed reciting the continents as I walk down our front steps, I barely notice Tucker Thomas leave his house.

On the sidewalk, I turn and see Tucker skip—skip!—down our shared front steps. It's the skip of a boy who knows he's going to get a hundred on today's test. It's the skip of a boy who doesn't need to take one last look at his globe before leaving the house. It's a pompous, arrogant, annoying skip!

I bet Tucker Thomas is not reciting the continents in his mind right now. He's probably thinking about where on the refrigerator door his mom and dad will hang his one hundred test paper when he gets it back.

"Bean," Tucker calls.

Why can't he use my first name like everyone else? At least he didn't use his other nickname for me, which I despise. I pretend I don't hear him.

"Hey, Bean," he yells again. "Ready for the test?"

"Am I . . ." I whirl around and glare.

Tucker's standing with his head tilted, a knucklehead grin on his face. "You know," he says, running a hand through his dark, wavy hair. "The geography test."

I shake my head in disbelief because that boy can be such a blooming idiot, and I walk toward school—away from him. I wish Nikki still lived on our street and she and I were walking to school together, like we used to. I wonder what terrible thing I did in a previous life to deserve to live next door to Tucker Thomas. I mean, why do our houses have to be attached so you couldn't fit a dime between them? Who cares about a dime, anyway? I wish there were a small country between us!

I glance over my shoulder and am disturbed to see Tucker hurrying toward me. I speed up. I'd be happy with the world's smallest country separating our houses—Vatican City.

Tucker closes the gap between us and walks beside me. "Hey, Bean," he says, catching his breath. "What European city has been called the birthplace of democracy?"

My heart does an extra panicked beat because I don't know which European city has been called the birthplace of democracy. I don't remember seeing that information in my notes.

"Give up, Bean?"

I keep walking, lips pressed together. Maybe Tucker's teasing me. Maybe that information was never given. Or maybe—gasp!—I wasn't paying attention when Ms. Lucas talked about that particular geography fact. Maybe I was thinking about Dad or Nikki or *Jeopardy!* or something much more important than the birthplace of democracy.

Tucker gets close to my ear. "Or do you know the answer, Bean, and are trying to rattle me?"

Rattle you? I wheel around, my hair smacking Tucker in the face. "Tucker, why are you following me?"

He blinks a few times. "Athens. The answer is Athens, Greece. You should know that, Bean." Tucker takes a step back. "And I'm not following you. I'm walking to school."

I cross the street.

Tucker crosses, too.

"Stop following me!" I stamp my foot, then walk forward with great purpose.

Tucker walks so closely behind me, I'm afraid he's going to step on the backs of my sneakers, like he used to do when we were in fifth grade together. "It's a free country," he says.

I turn around. "Stop."

He stops. "But I'm not following you, Bean."

"Yes, you are."

"No, I'm not," he says. "You just happen to be walking in front of me. And we're going to the same place."

I shake my head and see Matt Dresher approach. My stomach clenches. I can't stand that kid, but Tucker walks to school with him sometimes, which shows what a complete and total idiot Tucker Thomas is.

"You're so immature," I yell to Tucker, without looking back.

"You're so immature," he mocks.

"See," I shout. "That proves it."

"See," he says. "That proves nothing."

I breathe hard through my nose, but don't say another word. Tucker Thomas might have the brain of an MIT college professor, but he's about as mature as Charlie . . . when he's pretending to be Armpit Bacteria Man.

I jog the rest of the way to keep Tucker and Matt

Dresher at a safe distance. By himself, Tucker is annoying, but when he's with Matt, Tucker is downright mean.

When I get to school, I appreciate the fact that Tucker and I are in different homerooms. This will enable me to panic about the geography test in private—well, as private as a classroom with thirty-two kids, a teacher and a pet iguana can be.

Before going to his homeroom, though, Tucker pokes me in the shoulder from behind. "Good luck on the test, Bean," he says. "And don't forget we need to know the five oceans."

I nod. *Five oceans. That should be easy. I went over that this morning. There's the Pacific Ocean, the Atlantic Ocean . . . um, the Southern Ocean—I always forget that one—and the Indian Ocean.*

Tucker walks away.

Wait a minute. That's only four. What's the name of the fifth ocean? The Niña, the Pinta . . . oh, that's not it. "Um, Tucker," I call into the crowd of kids. "Tucker?" I whisper fiercely as I crane my neck to find him among the throng of kids. I push my glasses up on my nose and barely croak, "What's the name of the fifth ocean?"

But Tucker's gone.

And I'm alone in an ocean of middle school kids, not one of whom can prevent the geography disaster that's about to occur.

What Is the Red Umbrella?

Later, I walk into Ms. Lucas's room like my sneakers are made of lead (atomic number 82). My stomach is so discombobulated, it feels like I swallowed a porcupine. *Who invented tests, anyway? Especially geography tests? Why can't teachers assess our knowledge like they do on game shows? Then at least it would be fun.*

Tucker's already in his seat, leaning back with one arm casually laid over the desk behind him. His relaxed demeanor reminds me of how Dad used to look when he and I played along with *Jeopardy!* on TV. I bet a porcupine hasn't taken up residence in Tucker Thomas's gut.

I slide onto my desk chair, which is next to Tucker's—just like our houses are next to each other on Rutledge Street. Remembering my deficient store of geography knowledge in regard to the world's oceans, I whisper, "Hey, Tucker, what's the—"

"Everything off your desks," Ms. Lucas says.

My throat squeezes. *You can do this,* I tell myself. *Geography just isn't your thing, Butter Bean,* Dad says inside my head. *That's why you wouldn't do well on Jeopardy!* I gulp hard because I believe Dad. Then I slide my backpack under my chair, feeling like I'm about to get a tooth pulled, or at least get a rigorous and somewhat painful cleaning.

"A pen and nothing else." Ms. Lucas strides along the aisles. She taps Myrna Levin's desk. "*Everything off.*" Myrna tosses her tiny purse under her chair.

Ms. Lucas stands three desks in front of me, facing the front of the room.

I lean toward Tucker, eyes looking forward, and whisper, "What's the—"

"No talking," Ms. Lucas snaps, like she can see out of the back of her head. Either that or she has bionic hearing.

I sink low in my chair and cross my arms over my chest. My pen rolls to the floor, and I don't bend to pick it up, afraid I'll get in trouble again.

With lightning speed, Tucker snatches it from the floor and plants it on my desk.

Thanks, I think, too afraid to utter a sound, but impressed with Tucker's slick maneuver. *Why is he being nice to me?*

A paper lands on my desk. There are thirteen un-lucky questions on the front side and eight more on the back, including one essay question. *Gulp.* How will I have enough time to answer twenty-one questions—one of which is a totally unfair essay question about some tribe I've never even heard of? I don't think I know twenty-one things about geography all together.

"This exam is worth twenty percent of your grade for this marking period." Ms. Lucas's voice fills me with dread. "You may begin."

Those are the last words I hear before I pick up my pen, write my name and begin the process of flunking the test.

The first question is: Name the five oceans.

I glance at Tucker, who is hunched over his paper; then I write the four names I remember. Four, not five. Sweat breaks out in my armpits. I practically feel the 516,000 bacteria per square inch floating around in there.

Since Ms. Lucas is at her desk, I peek at my classmates. They are hunched over their papers, writing furiously. I'm sure each of them remembered all five oceans. I'm sure the kids in my class don't have Teflon-coated brains like mine when it comes to remembering geography facts. And I'm absolutely positive not one other person in this class, including Ms. Lucas and probably the entire school, has to deal with what I do: a dad who took off with her best friend's mom *and* her best friend, then moved to California, which happens to be on the opposite side of the country from me.

California borders the Pacific Ocean. At least I remember *that* ocean. I also remember that California is the most populous state in the country. One out of every eight people in the United States lives in California, including my dad, Stella Costelli and my former best friend, Nikki Costelli. The California coastline is 840 miles long. The state tree is the California redwood. Los Angeles, the largest of the 58 counties by population, happens to be where Dad, Stella and Nikki set up house.

Yup, I know the geography of California.

Wish I didn't.

I glance at the clock and realize I've wasted precious test-taking minutes thinking about Dad and what he did to me. For some reason, no matter how many times I think about it, the pieces won't fit together and make sense. Nikki was my best friend. Stella is her mom. How could Dad do something like that?

I return my focus to the paper on my desk. And I'm surprised that I know the next six answers after the oceans question. But then I get stumped on a question about the equator. I poke myself in the forehead a few times, but it doesn't jog any information loose.

As I sneak a peek at the class scribbling on their test papers, I remember a *Sesame Street* episode I watched a couple years ago with Charlie. He loved *Sesame Street*— used to sing the show's theme song in the bathtub. *"Sunny day sweepin' the clouds away . . ."*

In one segment, they showed a yellow boot, a yellow banana, a yellow sun and a red umbrella. Then they sang a song that asked which one didn't belong, which one didn't go with the others. Charlie said the banana didn't belong because you can't eat the other things. Smart kid. But the answer was the red umbrella, because the other objects were yellow. The red umbrella didn't belong; it didn't go with the others.

Right now, looking at this room full of kids who are probably writing all the correct answers on their test papers, who probably have best friends to hang out with and happy families to head home to after school, I feel like the red umbrella.

Who Is Phil and Why Doesn't He Wear Pants?

On my way home from school, Tucker catches up to me at the corner of Kindred and Rutledge, our street. He's chewing on something red and talks with his mouth full. "How'd you do on the geography test, Bean?"

I take a deep breath and consider sprinting for home. I could get there before him if I run the whole way, but for some reason I don't have the energy. "Okay," I lie. "How'd you do?"

"It was easy," he says, which makes me want to kick him. "You remembered the five oceans, right?"

"Right," I lie again.

"Name them," he says, practically bursting with conceit.

"The Atlantic," I say. "The Southern, the Indian, the

Pacific." And then I mumble something incomprehensible, hoping it sounds like the name of an ocean.

"Ha! I thought you might have missed one, Bean. It's the Arctic."

"Oh!" *That's it.*

"Lucas'll give you partial credit, though."

"You think?"

Tucker nods and stuffs a thick red licorice rope into his mouth. He doesn't offer me any. I wouldn't have accepted, anyway. He's probably had it in his pocket since last Halloween. Tucker's gross like that. His shirts are always 40 percent tucked in, 60 percent hanging out and 100 percent wrinkled. His hair always looks ruffled, like he uses his head as a Habitrail course for his hamsters, Gypsy and Rose. And Tucker always, always has a food product smeared across his shirt. Today, it looks like ketchup . . . or maybe it's red licorice slime.

We stop at the bottom of our steps. "So, what are you doing later?" Tucker asks.

The question startles me. Tucker never asks what I'm doing or where I'm going. He's usually too busy picking on me with Matt Dresher. And we haven't done anything together for about two years. *Why is he being nosy all of a sudden?*

"Um, I watch *Jeopardy!* at seven-thirty." I feel like a

dork, but it's the first thing that pops into my mind. Then, all at once, I'm mad at myself for sharing that bit of information with Tucker. *Jeopardy!*'s the one thing Dad and I always did together, our special tradition, and I didn't mean to tell Tucker about it. Although, he probably remembers that back when we were friends— when he used to be nicer—I'd go home every day at seven-thirty to watch *Jeopardy!*, no matter what we were doing.

"Cool," Tucker says, gnawing off another bite of licorice. "My grandma watches that show."

"Oh." Now I feel like an uberdork, knowing I have the same social life as Tucker's grandma.

"It's pretty funny," he says, chomping his licorice. "She won't even talk to us if we're at her apartment while it's on, and if we call between seven-thirty and eight on weekdays, she doesn't answer the phone. I think she has a crush on Alex Trebek or something."

I laugh before I can stop myself.

Tucker smiles.

My cheeks heat up. I can't believe I'm having a normal conversation with Tucker Thomas.

I press my lips together, determined not to say another word to him, but it's hard because Tucker says, "Talk to you later, Bean." Then he looks at me with his blue eyes. How come I never realized he had blue eyes? Pale blue, like a summer sky.

Eww!

I grab the key from the string around my neck and give a hard tug to snap me out of this. "Whatever," I say, and march up the steps to my house.

Tucker calls from the bottom step: "Watching *Jeopardy!* sounds way better than what I have to do tonight."

Wind whistles, and I watch gray clouds motor across the sky. I shiver and, against my better judgment, turn and ask, "What?" I think maybe Tucker and his blue eyes have to go to the dentist to get a tooth pulled or to the doctor to get a shot. But you don't do those things at night.

Tucker stands lopsided, like the weight of his backpack is too much for him. He almost looks like one of the cool kids. Almost. That's if one of the cool kids had a red stain a mile long across his shirt and a glob of something half-chewed showing in his mouth.

Tucker trudges up one step, stops and looks at me. "Dad's making me go to the Phillies game with him. Last game of the season."

A strong wind whips my hair, and I pick strands out of my mouth. "Baseball? With your dad?" I squeeze my house key till it bites into my palm. "Tucker, that sounds fun." *I'd do anything for my dad to take me to the Phillies game tonight.*

"Fun?" Tucker says, his cheeks turning as red as the licorice he's chomping. *"Fun?!"*

Tucker's anger surprises me. I take a step back, so I'm pressed against my front door.

"Bean," Tucker says. "On a fun scale from one to ten, baseball, for me, is a minus three thousand."

"Are you nuts, Tucker?" The one Phillies game Dad took me to was during the World Series. The World Series! And Dad took only me; Charlie had to stay home with Mom. As soon as we handed the guard our tickets and stepped inside the stadium, Dad bought me a green Phillie Phanatic doll—a plump creature with a snout like an anteater, who wears a Phillies jersey and baseball cap. Oddly, though, no pants.

I named my doll Phil. I still keep Phil on my bed and hug him every night before I go to sleep, even though somewhere along the way, Phil lost his jersey and he now has stuffing coming out of a hole under his armpit. I think Phil's adorable, even if he is almost the same color as the throw-up-green carpet covering my bedroom floor.

During the World Series game, Dad was hunched over in his I-can't-hear-you mode, but it was still great. The energy from the crowd was amazing. When the Phillies hit a home run, a Liberty Bell lit up and bonged,

bonged, bonged and the crowd went wild, waving their red and white towels above their heads. I held on to Phil's sneakered foot and waved him high above my head. It was the most fun I'd had with Dad since Disney World.

When the game was over, Dad rocketed out of his seat and punched his fist in the air. "Yes!" he shouted, and gathered me in a tight hug. He even hugged the people around us. Everyone did that, but I think Dad had a bet on the game. Judging from Dad's reaction when they won, it must've been a hefty bet.

After the game, Dad took me to the Country Club Restaurant—my favorite—and let me order anything I wanted, including a slice of lemon meringue pie and a vanilla shake.

How could any normal person not like doing that stuff with his dad? Then again, who said Tucker Thomas is a normal person?

I look at the glob of licorice puffing out Tucker's cheek and poking out of his mouth. It makes my stomach flop, and I have to look down so I don't get queasy. "Maybe you'll have a good time," I say, thinking that I'd trade places with him in a heartbeat. "That stadium is really fun. They have lots of stuff to do besides watching the game."

Tucker tilts his head like he's annoyed with me, clomps up the steps and faces me. "Bean, you've known me long enough to know baseball's my dad's thing. He wishes it were mine, but it's not."

Then Tucker shakes his head like I couldn't possibly understand what he's saying, pivots and disappears inside his house.

I feel empty, like the wind could blow right through me, which is completely ridiculous because Tucker Thomas and I aren't even friends anymore. We used to be great friends, going over to each other's houses all the time, but that was a long time ago—before my dad left and before the unfortunate hula hoop incident in fifth grade.

I stare at Tucker's closed door for a couple seconds, trying to comprehend what just happened. I decide, simply, that Tucker Thomas is an idiot.

Mr. Thomas is taking him to the last Phillies game of the season, and it's totally unfair. Tucker doesn't even want to go. *Take me.* Actually, what I really wish is that Dad were here and he would take me.

Even though I rarely miss a show, I'd miss *Jeopardy!* for that.

What Is Getting Let Off the Hook?

The smell of frying onions tells me Mom's home. I tiptoe toward the stairs, hoping I'll make it to my bedroom before she comes out and asks about the geography test I bombed.

My hand is on the banister when I hear "Livi? That you?"

Mom strides in from the kitchen, wearing an apron over her blouse and slacks. She wipes her hands on a small towel as she approaches. I know the first thing she's going to say is *How did you do on that test?* I want to forget about it. It's over. Damage done.

"Hi, Mom, I—"

"Listen, Livi," she says. "Neil's working at the library till nine."

I get a happy feeling inside. Neil working until the

library closes means Alex Trebek and I will have our date at seven-thirty without annoying interruptions. It means I get to answer all the questions myself without Neil distracting me or yelling the answers before I have a chance.

Mom steps closer. "I need to leave soon to cover a municipal meeting for the newspaper. Dinner will be ready in twenty. Okay?"

"Sure," I say, swallowing hard, waiting for Mom to ask about the stupid test.

"Okay, then." Mom nods and walks back into the kitchen.

I wonder why she didn't ask about the test. She *always* asks about tests, quizzes and homework, not to mention my pitiful social life, which consists of sitting at lunch with Brooke, Carly and Julia, who are best friends. With each other. They all live on the other side of town, so I *never* see them outside of school, and they always laugh at inside jokes I never understand. But at least I don't sit alone anymore. Lunch period went swiftly downhill after Nikki left. I wonder who she eats lunch with at her school in California. Probably a lot of really cool girls. And maybe even a few boys.

Mom pokes her head out of the kitchen. "One more thing."

"Yes?" I can't believe I almost want Mom to ask about the geography test now.

"Since both Neil and I will be out, you'll be responsible for Charlie until Neil gets home."

"That it?" I ask.

"Nope," she says.

Here it comes. I formulate the most positive answer I can. *I'm sure I'll ace the next test,* even though I'm sure I won't.

Mom says, "It would be a huge help if you could wash and dry the dinner dishes."

"The dinner dishes?"

"If you don't mind," Mom says, and heads back into the kitchen. "Thanks, Livi!" she calls. "You're a lifesaver."

Life Savers were invented in 1912 by Clarence Crane, a chocolate maker who wanted a candy that could hold up to summer heat better than chocolate. Pep-O-Mint was the first flavor created. Edward John Noble purchased the rights from Crane for a mere $2,900.

Sometimes, I wonder how my measly three-pound brain holds so much information. "No problem," I yell, and head up to my bedroom, thinking that at least I'm off the hook about my test . . . until the grade comes in.

But I also think it's a little strange that Mom didn't even ask.

What Is the Ugly Black Sock?

I'm assaulted by the brightness of my yellow room. I
wouldn't mind if it were painted mellow Big Bird yellow,
but this shade is obnoxious. It's like the sun . . . on ste-
roids. It's been like this since we moved in, and Dad always
promised he'd repaint any color I wanted, but he left before
that happened. And even after he's been gone two years,
my room is still a blinding reminder of things left undone.
I shield my eyes and wish I had a pair of sunglasses.

"Hi!"

I stumble backward. "Wh-what are you doing here?"

Charlie sits cross-legged on my vomit-green carpet,
racing Matchbox cars over piles of books. My trivia
books! He set them up like ramps and has a car in each
fist, zooming them over the covers and along the spines.

DJ, our orange tabby, is curled beside him. He opens

one eye to check out what's going on, then closes it again. Then he sneezes. *On my trivia books!*

"Absolutely not, Charlie Bean." I drop my backpack with a satisfying *whump* and bend to pick up the books. I put my face right in front of Charlie's and can see the freckles on his cheeks and the bridge of his nose. "You know not to touch my books. Do you want me to tell Mom?"

DJ stands, stretches and darts out of the room. *Smart cat.*

Charlie shakes his head so hard his fine hair flies around.

"Because I will," I say. "And she'll take your cars away. All of them."

He grabs my cheeks in his little palms. "Livi, no!"

I glare at him, even though it's hard to hang on to my anger with his damp palms pressed against my cheeks. "Then help me clean up."

He shakes his head again.

"What? You *want* me to tell Mom?"

"Uh-uh," he says. Then, in a tiny voice, "I want one."

"Huh?" I ask, fitting the trivia books back onto the shelf in size order.

He points to the books. "I want one."

I stop what I'm doing and look at my bother. "You want a book to race your cars on?"

He shakes his head. "To read."

I raise an eyebrow. Yesterday, when he read my Ripley's Believe It or Not!, he smeared chocolate on one of the pages. "You want one of my trivia books? To read?"

He nods so hard I think his head is going to fall off and plop into his lap.

"There's very little gross trivia in them, you know."

"I know," Charlie says. "I don't only like gross stuff, Livi. Just mostly."

I laugh. I can't help it. And I can't help but think Dad would be tickled to know that Charlie is turning out just like him. And me. Trivia addiction is definitely an inherited Bean gene.

Part of me wants to encourage Charlie to study trivia—to encourage him to do anything other than smash Matchbox cars into things and run around pretending to be Armpit Bacteria Man—but another part knows exactly the kind of condition my book will be in when it's returned. If it's returned.

In the past, when Charlie "borrowed" books from me, he's ripped out pages and spilled drinks on them. Once, years ago, when he was getting ready for his bath, he dunked my favorite book in the toilet, thinking it was waterproof like his bath books.

"I don't think so," I say. "You don't know how to take care of things."

Charlie crosses his skinny arms over his chest. "Then I'm not helping clean up."

I continue to replace books on my shelf. "I don't need your help."

"Please, Livi. I want to have a big brain like yours."

I suddenly don't feel so bad about my lousy geography test . . . or the fact that Dad's not here, taking me to see the last Phillies game of the season. "I don't have a big brain," I tell Charlie. "It weighs about three pounds, just like everyone else's." I ruffle his hair. "Knucklehead."

He grins, like calling him knucklehead was a big compliment.

A light goes on in my three-pound brain. I remember I have a series of boxed cards called Brain Quest on the shelf in my closet—too high for Charlie to reach—and they have tons of trivia for kids in different grades.

"Livi?" Charlie asks.

I've been staring off into space again. I have a tendency to do that when I think. I shake my head. "Charlie, I have something special for you."

Charlie's eyes grow wide. He touches my wrist with his sweaty hand.

"But it's not a book."

His shoulders slump.

"It's better than a book."

He sits tall.

I reach up to my closet shelf and check the boxes until I find the collection of questions designed for first graders. Charlie's only in kindergarten, so getting first-grade questions will make him feel smart.

"Got it." I sit on the floor with him and hand him the box.

Charlie runs his fingers over the words at the top and reads slowly. "'It's Fun to Be Smart.'" He shows me. "It's fun to be smart, Livi."

If only, I think, remembering Andy Baran kicking my chair in fifth grade and hissing at me to stop showing off, when all I'd done was answer most of the questions the substitute asked during the boys-against-girls Brain Blaster competition. Even though I helped the girls win, some of them whispered nasty comments, too.

"It sure is," I say, hoping it's a long time before Charlie has the awful feeling of answering a tough question in class and having kids stare like he just grew a third leg out of his butt and danced the hokey-pokey with it.

"Thanks, Livi!" Charlie clutches the Brain Quest to his chest and rockets out of my room.

Mission accomplished!

I finish putting my books away and get that empty feeling again. What's with me today? First, I feel empty when Tucker goes inside, then again when Charlie leaves. And I wanted him to leave!

I think I miss Dad.

If Dad walked through my bedroom door right now, I'd tell him how cute Charlie is, wanting to study trivia. I'd also tell him how stupid Tucker Thomas is because he doesn't want to go to a baseball game with his dad, and I'd remind Dad how much fun he and I had at the World Series game together. And I wouldn't, no matter what, mention how awful I did on my geography test. Dad already knows I'm lousy at geography. He doesn't need to be reminded.

I look at my bedroom door, almost expecting Dad to stroll in and say, "Hey, Butter Bean. What's kickin', chicken?" Of course, the door doesn't open, and that empty feeling inside my stomach expands and makes itself comfortable.

While I'm staring at the door, a soft *plink, plink, plink* sounds on my window air-conditioner. The plinks get faster and louder. Finally, rain splashes against my window in a deluge. "Perfect," I say, using my most sarcastic tone. Although I usually like the sound of rain, today it makes me feel like crying. I wonder if Tucker's baseball game will be rained out. That would make him happy.

I lie on my bed, staring at the obnoxiously bright yellow ceiling. Yellow like the sun . . . or a boot . . . or a banana. I grab Phil, hug him to me and listen to the rain—*plink, plink, plink*—like fierce teardrops splashing.

49

I sit up and hold Phil's fuzzy green hands. "If I miss Dad, I should call him. Right?"

Phil doesn't answer.

We have a calling schedule that Dad came up with. He calls once a week on Wednesdays . . . when he remembers. But I should be able to call my dad whenever I need him.

I roll off the bed and go into Mom's room to get the phone.

On the foot of Mom and Dad's bed is a sock. Neil's ugly black sock, with a hole at the toe. I pick it up with my thumb and forefinger, hold it out in front of me as though it's radioactive and drop it into the laundry hamper. That sock doesn't belong on Mom's bed. It doesn't belong anywhere in this house.

And neither does Neil.

What Constitutes an Emergency?

I sit on Mom and Dad's bed, away from where Neil's gross sock had been. I have the numbers to Dad's house dialed when Mom yells, "Dinner in five."

Pressing the phone to my ear, listening to it ring, I yell, "'Kay," hoping Dad doesn't pick up while I'm screaming.

"I'm reading," Charlie shouts, and I can't help but smile.

"Good for you," Mom yells. "Be down in five minutes."

"Hello?"

The voice coming through the phone catches me off guard. With the three-hour time difference, I didn't think *she'd* be home from school yet. Maybe she was sick today and didn't go in. Maybe her school gets out earlier than mine. Maybe . . . I bite my bottom lip. "Um, yeah, is my dad there?"

"Really?" Nikki says in a totally snotty way.

Yeah, really, I want to shout at Nikki. *He is my dad.*

Neither of us says anything, but I'm breathing hard. I hear Stella—Dad's second wife—in the background saying, "Who's on the phone, Nikki?"

There's a muffled sound. I chew on the edge of my thumbnail and consider hanging up—I have to go down to dinner in a few minutes anyway.

"Yes?" Stella says. "Who is this? If you're a telemarketer, we're on the do-not-call list and you shouldn't—"

"Hi, Stella," I say.

"Olivia?"

"Mm-hmm."

"Oh, hi, sweetheart," Stella says, fake cheer oozing through the phone. I picture her spiky heels, too-tight jeans, poofy blond hair and dangling earrings touching her shoulders. I feel like becoming an emetomaniac.

I imagine Nikki standing nearby, wearing jeans and a T-shirt. She never was one for being fake fancy, like her mom. Nikki liked things plain, except pizza, on which she loved extra mushrooms, onions and olives. I hate olives but was willing to pick them off my slices.

During the last summer break that Nikki was still

here, we made a lemonade stand in front of her house. She did cartwheels when cars drove by to draw attention to our stand. It worked! We used the profits to buy a pizza—extra mushrooms, onions and olives, of course—and soda and a new Monopoly game for our mega two-night sleepover.

Having my best friend live at the end of my block was great . . . until her mom (who'd already been divorced *twice*) and my dad (who wasn't divorced *yet*) decided getting married to each other would be a great idea. Without even asking how I felt about it, they got married in Las Vegas, then moved to Los Angeles to get a "fresh start."

And they took Nikki with them.

Nikki.

Not me.

"Hi, Stella," I barely croak into the phone, but in my mind, I think *Hi, stealer. Dad stealer. Best-friend stealer.*

"Did you want to talk to your dad, sweet pea?"

When Dad calls me one of his cute nicknames, it's affectionate and I like it. But when Stella does it, it makes me cringe.

"Is he there?" I ask, my voice small.

"Honey, I thought he was supposed to call you tomorrow night. Isn't that what you all agreed on?"

"Yes, but . . ." I wish I hadn't called. I should have

gone downstairs and helped Mom set the table for dinner. Then I wouldn't have been in her room getting the phone and wouldn't have seen Neil's ugly black sock. And I definitely wouldn't be talking to Stella the Stealer right now.

"He's in Vegas, sweetheart. Some tournament or other." I picture her waving a hand dismissively, her perfectly polished red fingernails slicing through the air. "He'll be home tomorrow. Want me to give him a message when he calls in?"

"No," I say, my mind reeling. Why does he "call in" to his second family, but not to us, his first family, his *real* family? "I can talk to him tomorrow," I say as though it doesn't matter. But it does matter. I don't want to talk to him tomorrow. *I want to talk to him now.*

"Sweet pea," Stella says, grating on my nerves, "he might be smack in the middle of something, but if it's real important, sugar, you go ahead and call on his cell."

I almost say *Dad told me not to call on his cell unless it was an emergency.* In fact, he told me three times. The last time, he yelled it. *What can Dad be doing that's so important, anyway? Especially in Vegas?*

"You still there, sweet pea?"

"Yes," I say, biting my bottom lip to keep from crying.

"Well, I'll be sure to tell your dad you called. You take care now, sweetie."

I hang up without saying *Thank you* or *Good-bye* or *I hate you*.

Dad should want to talk with me. Any time. Not just during his once-a-week phone calls to me and Charlie. Wanting to talk to your kids is part of being a dad.

I punch in Dad's cell number.

"Dinner!" Mom calls. "Livi, set the table. Charlie, put out cups."

Heart thumping, I cover the mouthpiece and yell, "Be right there."

"Now," Mom calls back. "I have to leave for work soon."

"Okay," I yell just as Dad answers.

"Yes?" he says.

"Dad?"

"Olivia? What's wrong? Is this an emergency? Is Charlie okay?" Dad doesn't sound concerned, just irritated.

"He's okay," I say, tears welling because of the mean tone in Dad's voice. "It's just that . . ." *Why did I call?*

"What is it, Olivia? I'm about to walk into a tournament."

"I—" I can't believe Dad doesn't want to talk to me because he's playing cards in Las Vegas. Tears threaten to breach the dams of my lower lids.

"Olivia?"

I don't say anything, afraid I'll cry.

"I can't talk now," Dad whispers fiercely. "I can't be late for this thing."

"Sorry," I say, even though I didn't do anything wrong. *Click*.

Not *So long*. Not *I love you*. Not *Tell your mother and brother I said hi*. Just *click*.

"Olivia, come down right now," Mom barks. "I already set the table. Your dinner's getting cold."

What Is Tucker Holding?

In our bathroom, I splash cold water on my face and stare in the mirror. My nose is red and puffy, like a clown's nose. Like an apple. Like a red umbrella.

I try to suppress thoughts of Dad, but they seep in and make my eyes leak. *Why wouldn't he want to talk to me, his only real daughter?* I swipe at my stupid eyes with toilet paper, then stalk downstairs. In the living room, I hear Charlie talking to Mom in the kitchen.

"The human scalp contains a hundred thousand hairs," he says.

"You don't say."

I picture Mom touching her own hair.

Charlie continues. "The average person uses the bathroom six times a day."

"I guess I'm way above average," Mom says.

"Huh?"

"Eat your vegetables, Charlie Bean."

I hear the sound of forks scraping against plates, and I sniff hard.

"Olivia?" Mom calls.

"One sec," I say, hoping to give my nose more time to return to its normal color.

In the front foyer, I stand on tiptoe and peek through the small window atop the door. Streetlights illuminate the rain-soaked sidewalk, making fat raindrops glimmer like diamonds on Mr. Thomas's silver Honda Fit.

I startle when I hear a noise next door.

Mr. Thomas charges down the steps, holding a folded newspaper—probably the one Mom writes for—over his head. I guess he's trying to keep his bald spot from getting wet. Mr. Thomas definitely does not have a hundred thousand hairs. His bald spot is nearly as large as the fifth ocean.

Beside his car, Mr. Thomas pivots and yells, "Hurry up, Tucker! It's not like I'm taking you to the damn dentist!"

I duck below the window, my heart stampeding. *That's what I thought earlier, that Tucker acted like he was going to the dentist.*

I hear *plink, plink, plink* as rain drums the aluminum awning over our front steps. I hear the clink of forks against plates in the kitchen. Then I hear another sound next door.

This time I stand to the side of our door's small window, straining to peer out without being seen.

Tucker walks down the steps like Charlie did when he was little, planting each foot firmly on the step before moving down to the next one. Tucker's acting like it isn't pouring outside. He's pretending his dad isn't waiting for him. *What is wrong with that boy?*

Mr. Thomas gets into the driver's side of his car and slams the door so hard the sound reverberates through our front door.

I duck to the side, my breathing quick and shallow, but I can still make out what's going on.

Tucker stands on the bottom step, twirling his umbrella.

If that were my dad, he'd probably drive away. *You snooze, you lose,* he'd most likely say. Not Mr. Thomas, though. He doesn't even start the engine. He simply waits. And Tucker keeps twirling his umbrella, like a total dork who doesn't realize how lucky he is to have a dad who wants to take him to a baseball game.

Finally . . . finally . . . Tucker reaches the sidewalk, and Mr. Thomas starts the engine. Tucker stands directly under the streetlight. Something registers with me as Tucker slips into the passenger side of the car. Mr. Thomas guns the engine and they pull away.

Tucker was twirling a red umbrella.

Who Is Acting Like Cro-Magnon Man?

In the kitchen, Charlie reads trivia cards at the table while absently pushing stir-fry around his plate.

"Eat up, mister," Mom says, grabbing her napkin and standing.

She raises an eyebrow at me. "Forget something, Olivia?"

"Sorry," I say. And I am. I'm sorry I wasted my time calling Dad when I could have been down here eating.

"Well, the stir-fry's cold." Mom gestures to my lonely plate at the table, then takes her plate to the sink. "Don't forget the dishes and make sure Charlie's in bed by eight-thirty. Okay?"

"Dishes," I say. "Eight-thirty." I slide onto my seat and dig into the stir-fry, eating around the celery—too stringy. Something about Tucker niggles at me, something I've never considered before. Maybe Tucker feels like I do sometimes, like he doesn't fit in. I mean, he walks to school with Matt Dresher sometimes and sits at lunch with a bunch of idiot boys who think it's hilarious to spout chocolate milk from their mouths like fountains and fling pudding at each other. (No wonder Tucker's shirt is always stained.) But when I see Tucker outside of school, he's usually alone. Maybe he feels—

"Olivia! Are you listening to me?" Mom waves a hand in front of my face. Her bracelets jangle.

Charlie giggles.

"Yes," I say. "I'll take care of everything. Go enjoy your meeting."

Mom slaps a palm on the table. "Olivia, no one enjoys municipal meetings. Not the people who have to be there. And certainly not the reporters who cover them. I just hope I'm not home too late." Then Mom mutters, "Guess I'm lucky to have a job, with what's happening at work."

"Guess," I say, still thinking about Tucker and wondering why I'm wasting precious gray matter on that boy when I could be doing something meaningful—like studying cool but useless trivia.

Mom kisses me and Charlie on the tops of our heads, grabs her bag and leaves.

I let Charlie ask me questions from the trivia cards

while I eat, but I don't pay much attention because I'm thinking about other things.

Besides Tucker Thomas and his red umbrella, I think about Neil's ugly black sock on Mom and Dad's bed. I stop chewing for a second and realize it's not Mom and Dad's bed anymore. Hasn't been for a long time. It's just Mom's bed. And . . . and . . . that's all I want to think about.

I shove a forkful of stir-fry into my mouth and re-member how mean Dad sounded on the phone, like I was bothering him. Like I, Olivia Bean, his one and only real daughter, was an annoyance who kept him from what he really wanted to do—gamble! The stir-fry goes down hard, and I'm pretty sure I swallow a gross chunk of stringy celery.

I never understood why Mom got so angry about Dad's gambling. Sure, he was kind of quiet when he lost, but when he won, he'd dance around the living room and take us out to dinner, and once, when Dad won a lot of money on a 54–1 horse race, he took us to Disney World for four days. Nikki joined us, and we had the best time ever.

But today, after hearing Dad's irritation because I called while he was at a tournament in Las Vegas, I understand why Dad's gambling might have upset Mom. When Dad focuses on gambling, he ignores everything else. I recall the Phillies game Dad took me to and my stomach cramps, because when I think about it—really think about it—Dad was so focused on the game that he didn't even notice when some drunk guy spilled his beer on my pants, and I had to walk to the bathroom *by myself* to clean it up. Mom would never have let me walk to the bathroom by myself at a stadium that big.

I shake my head, dislodging those unpleasant thoughts, because even with Dad's gambling issue, things were easier when it was just me, Mom, Dad and Charlie.

Charlie holds a trivia card close to his nose, and I wonder if he'll need glasses like I do. "Ben Franklin wanted the turkey to be our country's symbol," Charlie says, "but it's the eagle. Did you know that, Livi?"

"Yup."

"I wouldn't want to be a turkey, Livi. On our class trip to Pennsbury Manor, the kids laughed at the turkeys, like they were stupid birds." Charlie bites his lower lip. "They're not stupid, Livi."

"No, they're not," I say. "But I wouldn't want to be a turkey either. Especially at Thanksgiving."

Charlie giggles and plucks out a new trivia card. He seems so happy. He was so little when Dad left. Probably doesn't even care that we don't see him and that Neil has moved in. I bet Charlie doesn't even mind that Neil tries to act like our dad. But. He. Isn't!

The phone's ringing jars me from my thoughts. I'm glad for the distraction.

"Don't answer it," Charlie says, a bean sprout dangling from his lips. "Mom says we don't answer the phone while we're eating unless it's an emergency."

I grab the phone. "It's an emergency."

"Okay," Charlie says. "But the house isn't on fire and I'm not bleeding to death, so I'm telling."

I press the Talk button. "Hello?"

"Olivia?"

For one crazy second, I think it's Dad calling back to apologize, to say that of course I'm more important to him than some stupid gambling tournament. But it's not Dad. And I'm so disappointed my shoulders sag.

"What do you want, Tucker?" I ask, falling back into old habits, forgetting about his red umbrella and that maybe he feels like an outsider too. "I'm not supposed to answer the phone during dinner," I say, looking at Charlie. But really, I'm surprised Tucker called. It's something he hasn't done since we were friends a couple years ago.

"Oh, sorry," Tucker says. "But I—"

"Aren't you at the game?"

"No!" Tucker sounds super-excited. "On the way there, Dad heard on the radio that it was canceled because of rain. Isn't that great?"

I pay attention to the sounds of drumming rain and whooshing wind. "I guess." I don't say what I'm really thinking, which is that it's not great at all because Tucker's dad probably really wanted to go. Tucker is such a lucky butt and he doesn't even realize it.

"So, I was wondering," Tucker says. "If maybe you want to come over and watch *Jeopardy!* together."

I reel back, as if Tucker has reached through the phone and poked me in the eyes. "*Jeopardy!*—you? Tonight?" *Why am I talking like Cro-Magnon Man? Did Cro-Magnon Man even talk? His cranial capacity was larger than ours, so it's—*

"If you want to, I mean," Tucker says. "Of course you don't have to. If you want to watch it alone, to, you know, focus, I totally understand."

"I . . . uh . . ." I look at Charlie, who is sticking his tongue out with a piece of carrot on it. "I can't, Tucker. I have to watch Charlie tonight. My mom's working." I gulp. "And so is Neil."

"Oh."

He sounds disappointed. *Tucker Thomas sounds disappointed that I don't want to watch* Jeopardy! *with him tonight.* I'm pretty sure he's been taken over by an alien—a nice alien, who has both a brain *and* a heart.

I feel more comfortable when he's making fun of me,

65

calling me *Olivia Bean, Hula Hoop Queen* with Matt Dresher and making stupid gestures. Then at least I know how to react—nastily!

"Bean?"

"Yeah?"

"Maybe I can come over there and we can watch Charlie and *Jeopardy!* together."

My heart stops pumping its usual sixty to one hundred times per minute, or at least that's how it feels. "I, um, can't have anyone over when Mom's not home."

I imagine Tucker shrugging. "Okay. We can get together some other time."

My eyebrows arch. "Yeah," I say. "We do live next door to each other. I guess we'll bump into each other, um . . ." *Shut up, Olivia. Cro-Magnon Man was definitely smarter than you!*

"Okay." Tucker laughs. "Some other time."

My cheeks get warm. " 'Kay."

"Bye."

"Bye."

I click off the phone, but hold on to it for a long time.

"Livi?"

"Yeah, Charlie?"

"Why are you smiling?"

I touch my lips. "Am I?"

What's So Important About Getting on Kids Week?

When I finish drying the last dish, it's 7:24.

I think about how nice it will be to watch *Jeopardy!* without Neil shouting answers before I have a chance to think. I can't believe Tucker wants to watch *Jeopardy!* with me. Maybe he's tricking me, and once I went to his house, he'd slam the door in my face or call me names. But it didn't sound like a trick. How can Tucker make fun of me with Matt Dresher one minute and be nice to me the next?

In the living room, Charlie, wrapped in a towel, sits on a stool with water clinging to his eyelashes. "I washed up, Livi. I'm ready to watch *Jeopardy!* with you."

I press my lips together, barely holding back a verbal explosion. *I'm watching* Jeopardy! *by myself tonight!* Then I remember how Neil handled Charlie last night. "Listen, little man," I say, as calmly as I can. "*Jeopardy!* is my special thing. If you hang out in your room, playing cars or reading trivia while I watch *Jeopardy!* . . ."

Charlie leans forward, mouth open, waiting to hear how sweet a deal he's going to get.

"I will play any game you want when it's over." I glance at my watch. Two minutes till showtime. *Get out of here, Charlie!*

He tilts his head. "Even smash 'em racing cars?"

I check my watch. One minute. "Especially smash 'em racing cars. I love smash 'em racing cars." I have no idea what it is.

"But—"

"See you in half an hour." I push Charlie toward the stairs.

"Don't forget," he says, and runs upstairs, grabbing the banister with one hand and holding his towel up with the other.

I collapse onto the stool and flip on the TV. *Success!* When I hear the "Think Music," my shoulders relax. "This is *Jeopardy!*," the announcer, Johnny Gilbert, says. As he introduces today's contestants, I imagine myself behind one of the podiums, preferably the one farthest to the left—the returning champion's spot.

Alex Trebek strides onstage, and I think about Tucker's grandmother having a crush on him. I stop giggling when Alex reveals the categories in his smooth, confident voice. Contestants provide one question after the next, in rapid-fire succession.

A: Weighing around a ton, the eland is the largest species of this animal in the world.
Q: What is antelope?
A: In 1972 Frito-Lay introduced its nacho cheese flavor of these chips.
Q: What are Doritos?
A: The potato didn't originate in Ireland but in the valleys of this South American mountain chain.
Q: What are the Andes?
A: He had the dynamite idea to launch a new television network known as TNT.
Q: Who is Ted Turner?

Even though I'm by myself and can focus, I miss a lot of them. Either the answers are really tough tonight or the other junk swirling around my mind is short-circuiting my brain. *Tucker wants to watch* Jeopardy! *with me.*

During the commercial break after the first round, I give myself a good talking-to. This is *Jeopardy!*, after all. It's only one half hour out of the day. I can give it my full concentration. I roll my head from side to side. I feel like a boxer who was trounced during round one but is ready to get back in the ring and stomp some trivia butt. I feel like Joe Louis—the Brown Bomber—except I'm the heavyweight champ of trivia.

Bring it on, Alex Trebek!

I lean forward and shout out questions during the Double Jeopardy! round.

> A: Polenta is a dish of cooked, ground this.
> **Q: What is corn?**
> A: In 1917 the son of an Illinois book printer joined with a New York store and started this company.
> **Q: What is Barnes & Noble?**
> A: This character lived just north of Who-ville and hated roast beast (for a while).
> **Q: Who is the Grinch?**
> A: This organization sells up to eight varieties per year of its cookies, including these favorites: peanut butter sandwich, thin mint and shortbread.
> **Q: What are the Girl Scouts?**

I do better than the contestant on the right, who finishes with a humiliating $800. The guy in the middle doesn't do well either. He ends with only $4,600. But the returning champion has $28,800 so far. $28,800! And that's before the Final Jeopardy! round. He can't lose now, unless he's a complete idiot, bets all his money and doesn't know the final question.

I feel like I'm about to win that money. "You go!" I scream, and pump my fist.

"What?" Charlie calls downstairs.

"Not talking to you." *Hush!*

"Okay. Come up soon. I'm scared up here by myself."

"Be up soon," I yell. "Get our game ready." *And be quiet!*

"'Kay, Livi!"

I think about that amount of money: $28,800. That's a fortune for twenty minutes' work. It's like earning $86,400 an hour. And the only people who can do that are probably Bill Gates, Oprah Winfrey, Mark Zuckerberg and maybe some oil sheik from Kuwait. And possibly my dad, if he's having the best winning streak of his life at a high-stakes blackjack or poker table. My stomach gives a little twist at that thought.

"Is it time yet?" Charlie screams from upstairs.

"Not yet!" I shout. "Don't bother me until the show's over or I won't come up."

"Okay," he yells. "I won't bother you, Livi."

"You're bothering me now," I mutter.

The show's back on, and the contestants are thinking about their wagers. "Don't waste your time," I whisper to the two contestants on the right. "You don't have a chance."

That's when the phone rings. "No! *Jeopardy!* isn't over yet!" I say in a panicked voice, as though the person calling can hear me. It's times like these I wish we had a DVR to record shows, like normal people. But Mom says it's a waste of perfectly good money.

My mind whirls through possibilities. It could be Tucker again. But why would he interrupt the show? He obviously knows I'm watching it. It could be Mom, but she'd know better than to call during *Jeopardy!*, too, unless it was an emergency. Dad! It's the only thing that makes sense. He's probably calling to say he's sorry for being so mean on the phone with me earlier.

I grab the phone and almost say *Hi, Dad,* but catch myself. "Hello?"

"Oh, hi, Olivia."

My whole body deflates. "Neil, *Jeopardy!*'s on." I glance at the screen. The Final Jeopardy! round is starting.

"Sorry," he says. "What was I thinking?"

"Don't know," I say, staring at the screen and biting my thumbnail. "But it's definitely still on."

"Okay. I was just calling to see how you did on your geography test." A pause. "I guess I'll talk to you later."

I turn away from the TV screen, the phone pressed to my ear. Neil remembered my geography test. "Well, actually, not so great," I say. "I missed the fifth ocean and a couple other things."

"Ouch," Neil says, and sounds like he means it. "Don't worry, Olivia. You'll get 'em next time. Now go enjoy the end of your show."

Even after I hear the click . . . and the dial tone . . . I hold the phone to my ear. *Neil remembered my geography test.*

When I turn back to the TV, the show's over. I missed the Final Jeopardy! round. I can see by the defending champion's score that he won. Duh! He ends with $36,000, so he must have wagered $7,200 and answered correctly. I could have done that. Alex Trebek and the other players shake his hand. If that guy keeps winning, he'll be invited to the Tournament of Champions, where he can win megabucks.

I missed it—the best part of the show. Because of Neil.

"O-LI-VI-A!" Charlie yells. "You said . . ."

"Coming!" I snap.

I turn off the TV, and the phone rings. Again.

I figure it's Neil and he forgot to tell me something, but I hope it's Dad, calling to say he's sorry.

"Hello?"

"Did you see it?" Tucker is out of breath, like he ran up and down our front steps a dozen times.

"See what?"

He takes a big, wheezy breath. "I ran all the way to your house and—"

"All the way? Tucker, we live next door to each other."

"Yeah, right." He heaves a great breath. "But then I remembered . . . you said no one . . . could come over . . . when your folks . . . um, your mom isn't—"

"Tucker, get on with it!"

"Did you see *Jeopardy!*?"

"Of course I saw it, Tucker. I always—"

"Then you saw it!"

I want to go next door, grab Tucker by his stained shirt and shake him. "Saw what?"

"Bean, you're going to do it, aren't you?"

"Do what? Tucker, what are you talking about?"

"*Olivia!*" Charlie screams.

I cover the phone. "Be right there, Charlie. Please!" I hear him hopping, probably pretending to be Tigger from *Winnie-the-Pooh* or a pogo stick or Tigger on a pogo stick.

"Tucker?"

"Yeah?"

"What are you talking about?" I look at the ceiling,

knowing I have to get to Charlie soon before he does something stupid, like giving one of my trivia books a bath . . . in the toilet.

"Kids Week, Bean!" Tucker says. "There's an online test for you to try out to be on Kids Week!"

I pull the phone away from my ear and move my mouth to form words as my brain processes. "Kids Week?" I ask. "Are you absolutely, positively, without a doubt sure they announced Kids Week during the show?"

"Of course."

"Oh my gosh! I've been waiting for the announcement. It's my last chance." My heart feels like it's going to pound itself right out of my body, but a tiny part of my brain tells me this is a trick. How could I have missed an important announcement like that? Maybe that's why Tucker has been so nice to me. It would make it all the more nasty when he pulls a trick like this on me now and tells me it's a big joke.

"Listen, Tucker," I say, mean and snotty. "If you're tricking me—"

"Why would I do that?" he asks in a soft, innocent voice.

My brain feels like it's whirling inside a blender. *Why is Tucker being nice to me? Just last week, he and Matt made fun of me the whole way to school.* "Sorry," I say, realizing this isn't a trick. "I must've been on the phone with Neil when they announced it. What did they say, Tucker? Exactly."

"They're looking for contestants, ages ten to twelve. You're twelve, Bean. You've got to apply."

"Twelve. Right," I say.

"So have your mom go on the site and register you."

"Mom. Register," I say.

"Bean, you okay?"

"Yeah," I say. "Okay." But in my head, I'm thinking, *Kids Week. My last chance ever.* I don't tell Tucker that I took the online test last year and never got a call back, probably because of my geography deficiency. And I definitely don't tell Tucker I didn't get a chance to take the test when I was ten because that's when Dad left, and everything was a big mess back then.

Dad. Something wonderful pops into my mind. I feel like a balloon filling with helium, like I could float up to Charlie's room without using the stairs. All because of one detail that ping-pongs around my brain at warp speed—faster than the speed of light.

The detail is a geography fact—one I actually know: *Jeopardy!* is filmed in Culver City, California. Culver City is right next to Los Angeles. And Dad lives in Los Angeles.

I've got to get on that show.

What Is Patience?

I take the steps two at a time to get to the computer in Mom's room. I've got to check this out, read the rules and make sure Tucker's right. *Kids Week online test.* I can't believe it!

My hand is wrapped around the doorknob when Charlie yells, "Olivia, I've got everything set up. Come. In. Right. Now. Like. You. Promised."

I stop. I did promise. And unlike some members of the Bean family, I like to keep my promises. Especially to Charlie.

So even though what I want to do more than anything is go on the *Jeopardy!* site and find out about Kids Week tryouts, I let go of the doorknob and walk to my little bother's room.

"You're here!" Charlie's eyes go wide, and he wraps

his arms around my legs, pressing his cheek into my hip. "I thought you weren't coming, Livi." He sniffs. "I thought you were tricking me so I'd let you watch *Jeopardy!* by yourself." He kisses my hip. "But you're here!"

This makes it especially hard to do what I'm about to do. I know Charlie doesn't deserve this, but I have to because if I wait another minute, I'll burst. "Look, Charlie, I'm really sorry, but something important came up. Just now. And I can't play with you, even though I really, really want to."

He looks up at me, still gripping my legs ferociously, his wide eyes blinking, blinking, blinking.

"I'm sorry," I say. *Stop looking at me like that.* "Charlie, it's super-important."

"Will you be done in two minutes?"

I wince. "I may not be done before your bedtime, but I can try—"

"O-li-vi-a," Charlie whines. Then he looks at me, still blinking, until droplets roll down his cheeks. He doesn't even wipe them off. He just looks at me like he trusts me more than anyone in the world. I realize that he must feel exactly how I felt when Dad didn't have time to talk to me today. And I feel an ache in my chest the size of a football field—100 yards; 120, if you count the end zones.

Without a word, I plop onto Charlie's floor, cross-legged. I grab a metal dump truck and a miniature ambulance from the pile near his bed. "Okay," I say. "How do we play smash 'em?"

Charlie drops onto my lap, turns around and squeezes my neck with his bony arms. "You're the bestest sister ever, Livi."

Now, I have to blink, blink, blink to keep tears from falling.

What's the Significance of Twenty-Four Years?

By the time I tuck Charlie into bed and pull the blanket up to his chin the way he likes it, leave his door open five inches (because he's five) and turn on the hallway light, it's ten minutes *after* he's supposed to be in bed.

It takes about 1.2 seconds for me to get myself in front of Mom's computer. I never realized how slowly her computer loads. She'll need to fix that before I take the online test. I tap my foot and keep checking the door because I'm not supposed to be on Mom's computer without asking her permission. But this is too important to wait.

I scan the *Jeopardy!* site.

Tucker's right. They're looking for contestants for Kids Week. Even though a parent can register a child up until the test, which is November 3, about five weeks from today, I don't want to wait. Mom needs to register me now, just to be safe. I don't want to miss my last chance.

I turn off Mom's computer and get ready for bed, determined to stay up until she comes home so that I can ask her to register me tonight.

Reading trivia books usually relaxes me, but tonight my mind whirls as I wait in bed to hear the front door open. I think about Dad again, how short he was with me on the phone. I think about Charlie, and how happy he was that I played with him. But mostly, I think about Tucker, how he didn't want to go to the baseball game with his dad, how he wanted to hang out with me tonight. "Thank you, Tucker Thomas," I whisper, because I'm so glad he told me about registering for the Kids Week online test.

My stomach is twisted in knots by the time I hear the front door open. I leap onto my vomit-green carpet and have my hand on my doorknob when I hear it. Whistling. Neil's whistling.

I check the time: 9:35. And Neil's home, not Mom. I guess that meeting she was talking about is running late. Don't those municipal people know my future career as a contestant on *Jeopardy!* is at stake here?

A part of me wants to ask Neil if he can register me, even though he is definitely *not* my parent. But another part doesn't want Neil involved with this. With *Jeopardy!* It's a special thing between me and Dad, and no one invited Neil to be included.

I plop onto my bed, stare at the blindingly yellow ceiling and hug Phil to my chest. At 10:15, Mom's still not home. She must be covering the world's longest municipal meeting.

I turn off my light so that when Neil comes upstairs, he'll think I'm asleep and won't come in to check on me or say goodnight. In the darkness, I force my eyelids open. I don't want to fall asleep before Mom gets home.

Must. Stay. Awake.

My eyelids feel like sheets of granite and keep drooping, even though I tell them to stay open.

I must have fallen asleep, but when I hear the front door open, my eyelids spring up like window shades. It's 11:47.

I slip out of bed, tiptoe along the vomit-green carpet and open my door a crack.

I hear Neil's voice. "Welcome home, baby."

Then an odd sound.

And Neil again. "Marion, what's the matter? What's wrong, honey?"

Neil sounds like he's talking to a little kid who's come home bloody and bruised. My heart pounds like crazy. Is Mom hurt? Was she in a car accident?

I resist the urge to charge downstairs. Instead, I strain to hear through the opening between my door and the doorframe.

Mom is talking fast, but she's blubbering at the same time, so there's no way I can understand what she's saying.

I open my door an inch farther and hear Neil's soft words. "It'll be okay, Marion. We'll figure this out. We're a team now."

We're not a team, I want to shout. *You're just a substitute player. Mom, Charlie and I are the team. You're not even a lowly batboy on this team, mister!*

"Come on," I hear Neil say. "Let's get you a nice warm bath." His voice gets louder. "You'll feel better."

I hear Mom sniff and realize they're at the bottom of the stairs.

I leap into bed and pull the covers up to my chin.

Right outside my bedroom door, I hear Mom crying softly and Neil saying, "It'll be okay. I'm telling you, Marion, it'll be okay."

"How can anything be okay"—Mom sniffs hard— "after twenty-four years?"

Twenty-four years? What's twenty-four years? Someone's age? Twice as long as I've been alive?

My questions don't get answered because the bathwater runs and I can't hear anything else they say.

What will be okay? I clutch Phil to me. *What's wrong with Mom? What does any of it have to do with twenty-four years?*

I stay up a long time, worrying and straining to hear more clues.

But after the bathroom door finally opens, Mom's bedroom door opens and closes and I don't hear another thing.

Who's a Poet and Doesn't Know It?

In the morning, I throw on clothes and rush downstairs. The smell of buttery pancakes and maple syrup wafts from the kitchen. How can Mom be making pancakes when she was so upset last night?

In the kitchen, Charlie's at the table, running a Matchbox car over the lone pancake on his plate. He stops and looks at me. "Hi, Livi."

"Hey, Charlie," I say, then turn my attention to the pancake-flipper standing by the griddle. "Neil?"

He whirls around, spatula in hand like a talisman. There are deep wrinkles between his bushy eyebrows—a telltale sign of worry. "Hey, Olivia," he says, forcing a smile. "Your mom's still sleeping, so I made you and Charlie pancakes."

Mom's usually up with us in the morning, even if it's

been a late meeting night and she can barely prop her eyelids open. She always packs Charlie's lunch bag for kindergarten and gives me suggestions for what I should put in mine. I look at the counter and see our two lunch bags already prepared.

I tilt my head at Neil. I want to ask what's wrong with Mom, but Charlie's playing with his cars, and I don't want to upset him. So I take a plate with two pancakes from Neil and join Charlie at the table.

"How come you get two?" Charlie whines.

"You can have another one when you finish that one, champ," Neil says.

It makes the hairs on the back of my neck rise when Neil acts like he's our dad. I almost give Charlie one of my pancakes, but I know he wouldn't eat it anyway. Grandma Sylvia used to say Charlie eats like a bird, but that's not right because most birds eat half their body weight every day. Charlie barely eats anything, unless it's made from sugar and chocolate, of course.

Charlie shrugs and goes back to rolling his toy car over his pancake.

Neil brings his own plate over with one small pancake. He usually eats piles of food, along with coffee and juice. Not today.

What's going on? I want to scream, but I shove a bite

of pancake into my mouth to keep myself quiet for Charlie's sake.

Neil must see the worry on my face because he touches my shoulder, looks right at me and nods, like everything's okay. But this gesture actually makes me more nervous.

Charlie doesn't seem to notice anything.

Since we really can't talk about what happened last night in front of Charlie, I decide I'd better talk about the other thing.

"Neil?"

He looks up, surprised, like I yanked him from his thoughts. "Yes?"

Charlie looks up, too.

"Um, there's this thing called Kids Week on *Jeopardy!*"

"Yeah, where the kids compete," Neil says. "I've seen that before."

"Well." I stab a piece of pancake. "They're looking for contestants now."

Charlie blurts out, "Livi, you could do that. You could do a contest on *Jeopardy!*" He rockets out of his chair and hugs me, pressing his cheek against mine.

When he goes back to his seat, I wipe sticky syrup off my cheek, wondering how he got syrup on his cheek without eating any of his pancake.

"Thanks, Charlie. I want to be on it."

"So . . . ," Neil says, his bushy eyebrows raised.

"Here's the thing." I put my fork down. "A parent has to register me. A parent. So—"

"And you want to try out," Neil says, nodding. "You want to try your hand at getting on *Jeopardy!*"

"Well, yeah," I say, feeling a little embarrassed and not sure why.

Neil leaps out of his seat and hugs me, too. "Livi, I think that's terrific. Good for you."

I'm stiff as a board while he hugs me.

Neil sits back in his chair and saws into his puny pancake. "Olivia, if anyone can do this, you can."

"Last year I tried, but I never got called back. Maybe I didn't do as well on the test as I thought. There was that pesky geography question and a couple other stumpers." I shove a piece of pancake into my mouth. "Or I did okay on the test and they didn't pick me because a lot of kids try out. A lot!"

Neil stares at me, not eating, just focusing completely on what I'm saying. It's weird; I can't remember Dad ever doing that—giving me his full attention.

I think about Mom crying last night, and I feel bad for talking about signing up for *Jeopardy!* when something is obviously upsetting her. I heard Mom cry once before. Once. After Dad left. And that was in her room, when she probably thought I couldn't hear. So the fact that she was crying last night is a big deal.

"You'll win," Charlie says.

"Thanks, Beanpole," I say.

He shrugs and looks into my eyes. "You'll win, Livi," he says again, like he's a pint-sized fortune-teller.

I get a funny tingle down my spine.

"Olivia," Neil says, stuffing a piece of pancake into his mouth. "This sounds like a great idea. What do you have to do?"

"Nothing. Just take a test online. Well, to start."

"Sounds simple enough," Neil says.

"Sounds simple enough," Charlie repeats, not looking up from the toy car rolling over his pancake.

I gulp. "It's just that I'm twelve now. That's the oldest you can be." I wish Mom were sitting here instead of Neil. "And I don't want to miss my chance."

"Why would you miss it?" Neil asks.

"Miss it. Kiss it. Fiss it," Charlie sings. "Biss it. Wiss it. Hiss it."

Neil looks at Charlie and shakes his head. "A poet and doesn't know it."

Charlie smiles. "I'm a poet, Livi."

"Yeah, I heard."

"Heard. Nerd. Derd. Ferd. Blerd," Charlie says.

"A parent has to register me," I say. "The sooner the better."

"What's the deadline?"

My stomach twists. "The test is on November third and you can register practically right up until the test, but . . ."

"Test. Messed. Nest. Best. West," Charlie sings.

"But?" Neil asks.

"I'm a poet," Charlie reminds us.

"But I don't want to wait," I say. "I want to be registered right away. I don't want to take any chances."

Neil nods. "Just tell your mom about it after school. I'm sure she'll—"

"But she'll be at work," I say.

Neil looks at his plate, clears his throat and runs a hand through his thick hair. He doesn't say a word.

What's So Funny, Tucker Thomas?

I'm still thinking about what Neil *didn't* say this morning when I walk down our front steps.

Tucker explodes from his house and runs down the steps behind me. "Hey, Bean."

"Hey," I say, remembering Tucker's red umbrella yesterday and feeling grateful for the distraction from worrying about Mom.

"Your mom register you for Kids Week yet?"

Even though it's cool outside, my cheeks grow warm. *So much for getting a break from worrying about Mom!* I want to tell Tucker it's none of his business. But I remember he invited me over to watch *Jeopardy!* yesterday and called to tell me about registration, so I shake my head. "Not yet."

"She'd better do it soon," he says, hoisting his

backpack onto his shoulder and walking beside me. "Don't want to miss your last chance, right, Bean?"

"She'll do it," I say, wishing he'd stop talking because it makes me think about last night and how Mom was crying. *What could it be?* The way Neil was silent after I mentioned Mom being at work, I wonder if it has something to do with that.

When we get to the end of our street, Matt Dresher walks toward us from the side street. I shrink into myself and slow my pace. *Great! Just what I need now.*

"Hey, Thomas!" Matt calls.

I allow myself to fall several steps behind Tucker. *Please don't notice me.* Maybe I could run ahead. Maybe—

"Bean!" Matt shouts, nodding toward me.

I nod slightly and walk faster—way faster—pulling ahead of Tucker and Matt. Behind me, Matt calls, "Hey, Olivia Bean, Hula Hoop Queen."

I cringe.

"Come back here, Olivia Bean, Hula Hoop Queen. I want to see your great hula hoop routine." He laughs a loud, obnoxious laugh.

I keep walking fast. While I hear Matt laughing, I picture him thrusting his hips from side to side, pretending to be hula hooping, like he usually does when he sees me. Tucker does the stupid motion too. And sometimes he also—

Tucker bursts out with his obnoxious, horselike laugh. He sounds like he's choking. I wish he were! *What's so funny, Tucker Thomas? How could you be so nice to me yesterday and so mean to me today?*

I glance back and see Tucker doubled over with laughter. Matt is pointing at me and holding his stomach because he's laughing so hard. I can't believe Tucker, who was so sweet to me yesterday, is laughing with such gusto about my unfortunate hula hoop incident.

Now I remember why I can't stand that boy!

I huff to school, the sounds of their laughter fading behind me. But I can still hear Tucker's horse-like guffaw in my mind. The unfortunate hula hoop incident was *not* funny. Why can't Tucker understand that I don't want to be reminded of it? And why does something about the incident keep nagging at me, even though I can't figure out what it is?

I shake those thoughts from my mind and walk as fast as I can without actually running. I have more important things to think about than Tucker Thomas and Matt Dresher. I need to think about registering for the Kids Week test. I also need to remember to make Carly a card; her birthday is tomorrow. Brooke and Julia will probably get her really nice presents with store-bought cards, but Mom said we can't afford to give presents unless I'm going to a birthday party. And Carly's not having a party this year. Instead, her parents are taking her to Disney World. Lucky butt! Disney World would be way more fun than worrying about registering for the *Jeopardy!* test and wondering what's going on with Mom.

What is going on with Mom?

Why Is Charlie Watching TV on a School Day?

At school, I avoid Tucker.

I don't even look at him during lunch when I walk right past his table. As usual, I sit with Carly, Brooke and Julia, even though instead of including me, they talk with each other about some club they've joined, where they learn a foreign language and then, at the end of the year, travel to a country where that language is spoken.

"Do you know anything about Bolivia, Olivia?" Carly asks.

"Ha, that rhymes," Julia says.

"Yeah, it does," Carly says, sitting taller, like she's proud of herself for rhyming something with my name.

Brooke bumps against Carly with her shoulder. "You're *not* a poet and we all know it."

Julia laughs so hard she sprays the table with cookie crumbs.

I'm a little grossed out and have no idea what's funny, so I answer Carly's question about Bolivia. "I don't really know anything about Bolivia," I say, nibbling on the peanut butter and jelly sandwich Neil put in my lunch bag. "I'm bad at geography."

Julia shakes her head. "Olivia, you know everything."

"About everything!" Brooke adds.

"Not everything," I say. I don't want anyone to think I'm showing off. That's why I lied and said I don't know anything about Bolivia. It's a relatively poor landlocked country in South America that the Andes Mountains run through. Just because my brain works like an encyclopedia doesn't mean I have to sound like one.

Why would they want to go to Bolivia? They've never mentioned wanting to go there before. If they're going to spend all that money to travel somewhere, they should go someplace that matters to them.

The only place I care about traveling to is Culver City, California. That place really matters to me for two reasons. *Jeopardy!* is filmed there and it's right near Dad. And Nikki.

Nikki.

If she were here now, she'd share her Tastykakes with me, and I'd share my baby carrots and apple slices with her. We'd talk about important things, like breaking a world record together or running in a marathon or how we'll become totally famous when we grow up and move into an apartment together in New York City. We'd plan our next epic sleepover, which would definitely involve pizza, with loads of toppings, and Monopoly. I haven't been invited to one sleepover since Nikki left.

Carly pulls eight bottles of nail polish from her purse. *Eight!* "This one is Tiger-Eye Orange and this one is Shimmer Like a Star Silver and . . ."

I yawn and glance over at Tucker but turn my head the moment he notices me.

Why can't that boy be nice to me *all the time* and forget about the unfortunate hula hoop incident once and for all? The last thing I need now is for that whole *Olivia Bean, Hula Hoop Queen* thing to erupt again at school. It took until after winter break in sixth grade for kids to forget about it and pick on someone else—Clarisse Matthesen, to be precise, because she left for winter break with perfectly clear skin but returned with a face full of acne. I owe Clarisse a huge debt of gratitude. She was nice enough to draw attention away from me. And someday, Clarisse's acne will clear up and she'll have lovely skin, but the memory of my unfortunate hula hoop incident will live on in kids' memories forever.

When the final bell rings, I dash out of school like a cheetah, the world's fastest land animal.

"Wait up, Bean!" Tucker calls as I rush toward home.

I do not wait. I hunch my shoulders and hope he's not with Matt Dresher.

"Bean!" Tucker calls again, sounding out of breath.

I don't stop. I break into a jog, my backpack pounding against my spine with each step.

"Bean!"

I jog faster because I don't have time for Tucker's teasing today. I've got to get home and call Mom to ask when she can register me for the test. And I need to find out why she was crying last night. *Please let her be okay!*

At our door, I notice Tucker is all the way at the end of the block. I'm glad I was able to outrun him.

Unfamiliar voices come from inside our house. I turn my key and push open the door, expecting to see a bunch of people sitting in the living room. My heart pounds from jogging . . . and worry.

But it's only Charlie, watching TV—that's where the voices came from. But that's weird because Charlie is supposed to be in aftercare at school. It's Wednesday. Mom always works till five-thirty on Wednesdays and Fridays, then picks Charlie up from aftercare.

And Mom *never* lets him watch TV during the school week.

"Hi, Charlie."

He raises one hand without turning from the screen. "Hi, Livi. This is good."

He's watching some violent cartoon. "It doesn't look good," I say, knowing Mom wouldn't want him watching this.

"It is," he says, still not looking up.

"Why are you home and where's Mom?"

Charlie shrugs, not turning from the screen.

"Earth to Charlie," I mutter, dropping my backpack and walking upstairs.

Mom's bedroom door is closed. But the bathroom door swings open, and Neil walks out. *Neil?* He's definitely supposed to be at work. *What's going on?*

Neil startles when he sees me; then puts a finger to his lips and whispers, "Your mom's sleeping, Olivia. She doesn't feel good."

"But—"

"I'm sure she'll be out soon. No worries." Neil opens the bedroom door and disappears inside.

I stand in the hallway, wondering what to do while listening to Charlie's stupid cartoon downstairs. *No worries?* Mom was crying last night. Today, she and Neil are not at work, and Charlie is watching TV on a school day.

I'm worried!

What's Going On with Mom?

Neil was wrong.

Mom doesn't come out soon.

Charlie ends up watching TV the rest of the day, except for when I make him come into the kitchen and give him SpaghettiOs and a sliced apple for dinner. I let him watch *Jeopardy!* with me, then get him ready for bed and tuck him in.

"Where's Mom?" Charlie asks.

"She went to bed early," I say. "She doesn't feel good." I tuck the blanket up to his chin, hoping he doesn't ask any more questions.

He doesn't.

"Don't forget the hall light," he calls.

"I never forget the hall light."

While I'm in the kitchen, washing the couple dishes from dinner, I hear a door open upstairs and someone walk downstairs. I hold my breath, hoping it's Mom.

"Hi, Olivia," Neil says, carrying two mugs into the kitchen.

"Hi," I say, holding back a flood of questions.

Neil places the mugs in the sink next to the empty SpaghettiOs can. Then he puts his big, hairy hand on my shoulder, which worries me so much that I forget to jerk away to remind him he's not my dad. "Look, Olivia, your mom still doesn't feel good."

"What's wrong?" I pull back just enough that Neil drops his hand.

Neil rubs his beard before answering. "She'll be fine. Absolutely fine, but she needs a little more time to—"

"Time for what?"

"She asked me to tell you she needs a little more time by herself. That's all. Okay?"

"Okay," I say, even though it's not.

I bite my bottom lip and watch Neil gather two bananas, a package of graham crackers, two plastic cups and a pitcher of water from the fridge. I listen to the sounds of him walking up the stairs and the bedroom door opening and then closing.

That's when it hits me. Mom isn't spending time

alone. She's with Neil. After Dad left, when Mom felt upset or sick, she'd come to me and ask for a hug. Me. Not Neil.

I leave the empty SpaghettiOs can in the sink and trudge upstairs, glaring at Mom's door before retreating to my room. I plop onto my bed, hug Phil to me and open a trivia book, but don't look at the words. I want to knock on Mom's door, but Neil's in there with her, and I have a feeling it's not the right thing to do.

I force myself to read trivia and then do homework. Mom's bedroom door still doesn't open, so I change into pajamas and turn out my light.

I stay up a long time, lying there with only light from the hall seeping in, listening for sounds or voices, but I don't hear anything. Someone goes to the bathroom, but that's it. That's all I hear the whole night.

While I'm lying in bed, I remember something that doesn't make me feel better. And even though it's late, I'm sure I'll never fall asleep.

It's Wednesday. Dad's night to call. And he never did.

Who's the Mom Here?

I guess I fall asleep eventually, because when I open my eyes, sun streams into my room, bouncing off bright yellow walls. I need to quit waiting for someone else to do it and paint my room a less obnoxious color.

But thinking about the color of my walls will have to wait. I have more important things to obsess about right now.

First I have to find out what's going on with Mom and make sure she's okay. Then I need to get her to register me for Kids Week.

I roll out of bed and shuffle into the hall, hoping things will be back to normal, but Mom's bedroom door is still closed and it's too quiet.

I peek into Charlie's room and can't believe he's not

up yet. Mom usually has him up and moving before I even open my eyes.

I shake Charlie awake, pick out some clothes for him and tell him to hurry so he doesn't miss his bus. Then I run down to the kitchen to fix us both a bowl of cereal and cut up the last banana to put on top, like Mom does. Then I pack Charlie's lunch and mine—peanut butter and jelly sandwiches with nothing else, because no one bothered to go to the market.

I don't like having to do all this work. It's Mom's job. Or Neil's. Not mine.

I still have to get ready for school myself. And I have a right to know what's going on.

While I'm fishing in the drawer for spoons for our cereal, I get an idea about signing up for *Jeopardy!* "Hurry, Charlie!"

He motors into the kitchen.

"Your pants are on backward," I say.

He looks down, nods and wiggles out of them. "Pants are hard sometimes, Livi," he says as he struggles to put them on the right way.

"Lots of things are hard sometimes," I say.

After I rush through my cereal and try to hurry Charlie—impossible—I leave the dirty bowls in the sink because I shouldn't have to do everything. I get Charlie to the bus, then come home, grab my measly lunch and backpack, lock the front door and wish I understood what Mom has been doing in her room all this time.

Tucker doesn't burst from his house like usual, and I realize it's because I'm late. I have to jog the whole way to school, my backpack slamming against my back with every step. To take my mind off everything, I think about how I'll execute my *Jeopardy!* plan.

During lunch, I go to the media center and ask Ms. Marchetto if I can use the computer.

"Of course, Olivia," she says. She's used to me coming in to read almanacs, Guinness World Records books and science magazines.

Ms. Marchetto points me to terminal number five.

It takes exactly three seconds to learn that the *Jeopardy!* site is blocked by the school's filter. The *Jeopardy!* site? I've seen Matt Dresher play some violent game on there once, and I can't access the *Jeopardy!* site? *Brilliant filter!*

I turn off the computer, grab my backpack, thank Ms. Marchetto and trudge back to the lunchroom to sit at a table by myself—can't deal with Brooke, Carly and Julia today—and worry about not getting registered. I was going to do it on the school computer. Even though it says a parent is supposed to register you, I figure they'd never know if I did it myself. At least, I hoped they wouldn't.

Well, that plan's shot. I'll have to wait for Mom. *Please be okay.*

I make up my mind that if Mom's not out of her bedroom when I get home, I'm going in.

Is No News Bad News?

Except for DJ curled on the couch, no one's in the living room when I get home, and the TV isn't on.

"Hello?" I call.

"Hi, Livi," Charlie yells from upstairs.

"Is Mom home?" I ask, grabbing the banister, knowing she must be home because Charlie wouldn't be here alone. DJ leaps off the couch, rubs his whiskered cheek against my pant leg, sneezes and darts toward the kitchen. I drop my backpack and start up the stairs.

"Yup," Charlie calls. "She's sleeping. Do. Not. Disturb."

"Do not . . . ?"

"*Disturb!*" he yells at the top of his voice.

"All-righty then," I say, tiptoeing the rest of the way up and pressing my ear against Mom's bedroom door. I hear nothing but soft breathing. I'd planned to storm in there to find out what's going on, but that doesn't seem like a good idea now that I'm actually here. I decide to let Mom sleep and I go into Charlie's room instead. He's got Matchbox cars and trucks in piles on the floor.

"Hi, Livi."

"Hi, Charlie. Did Mom say anything?"

Charlie shakes his head. "She picked me up, then said she's going to take a nap. 'Do. Not. Disturb.'"

"Did she look okay?"

"Her eyes were puffy and pink."

Maybe Mom has pinkeye and doesn't want us near her because it's contagious.

"Want to play with me, Livi?"

"Not right now," I say, and back out of Charlie's room.

Downstairs, I dump DJ off the kitchen counter, grab a glass of water and realize it's a good sign that Mom picked up Charlie. It means she's feeling well enough to get out of bed and drive. But I wonder when she's going to come out of her room. And register me for *Jeopardy!* I'll feel so much better when I actually see her.

In the meantime, if Mom's napping and can't register me, I know someone who can. The rules say a parent has to register you.

I pick up the phone.

Dad's a parent.

What's the Worst Phone Call?

Charlie walks into the kitchen and tugs on the bottom of my shirt before I have a chance to punch in Dad's number. "Play with me, Livi," he says. "I'm boring."

"You mean you're bored?" I ask.

"Yes," he says, yanking on my shirt. "Play. With. Me!"

I pry his fingers from my shirt, wave the phone at him and say, "Not right now."

Charlie's shoulders bob and he blinks. I put the phone down. I can tell Charlie's about to cry, and I can't ask Dad about *Jeopardy!* with Charlie crying.

"Hey, bud," I say. "Guess who I'm calling?"

Charlie shrugs and looks away.

I tug on the belt loop of his pants. "Come on, Charlie," I say. "Guess."

He tilts his head, looks at me and says, "Tucker Thomas?"

"What?"

"You know, Tucker Thomas."

"I know Tucker Thomas," I say, touching the note in my pocket that Tucker handed me when we passed each other in the hall this morning.

> Olivia Bean, Hula Hoop Queen—
> Why don't you smile?
> Just for a while?
> It makes your face look less mean.

"Tucker Thomas is a poop!" I say.

Charlie giggles. "Tucker Thomas is a poop."

"Yeah," I say, scrunching up Tucker's note and throwing it into the trash can. "A big, smelly poop."

Charlie dances around the kitchen, singing, "Tucker Thomas is a poop, poop, poopity poop."

"Hey, maybe you should take your show on the road," I say, which makes me think of Dad. If only Charlie would stop singing about Tucker Thomas being a poop, poop, poopity poop, I could call Dad and ask him. I grab Charlie's skinny wrist, not to hurt him, just to get his attention, and turn him around so that he's looking at me. "I'm calling Dad."

Charlie's eyes light up. "Dad? I want to talk to him. He didn't call yesterday when he was supposed to."

I reel back. "You knew that?"

Charlie nods. "He's supposed to call on Wednesdays."

"Right you are, little man." My heart squeezes and I feel a surge of rage toward Dad. "Yeah, he forgot." *Again.*

"Dad is a poop," Charlie says.

I laugh so hard, I need to wipe my nose with a napkin. "Yeah," I say. "Sometimes he is."

Charlie crosses his skinny arms across his chest, looking satisfied with himself.

"Well," I say. "I need to ask Dad something important, but when I'm done talking to him, I'll give the phone to you. Okay?"

Charlie nods so hard I think his head will drop to the floor. "'Kay, Livi." He yanks on my shirt again. "Hey," he says, as though he just got this great idea. "Maybe Dad will come for a visit soon. Maybe he'll take us to Disney World again. Wouldn't that be so cool?"

"You remember that?" I ask. "You were really little."

Charlie nods. "I threw up on the teacup ride."

I laugh. "You did throw up on the teacup ride. Dad spun the wheel too much and made you dizzy."

"Yeah, and some people came and cleaned it up, and then—"

"And then, when you felt better, Dad bought you a banana split with three scoops of ice cream."

Charlie nods. "Even though Mom told him it was a bad idea."

"Even though," I echo.

Charlie licks his lips. "I ate the whole thing."

"And you threw up again."

Charlie giggles. "That was fun. Livi?"

"Yeah, Charlie?"

"Rats can't vomit."

"Oh," I say, taken aback by that little gem of trivia. "I'm calling Dad now."

Charlie plops onto the floor, cross-legged. "I'm ready."

I punch in Dad's number, hoping Stella doesn't answer. I wouldn't mind hearing Nikki's voice, even though last time I called she wasn't nice. I miss talking to her. If things were normal now and we were still friends, she'd probably tell me not to worry about Mom. She'd say Mom is one tough lady and she'll be fine. And she'd help me study for the *Jeopardy!* test by quizzing me during lunch and after school. Nikki would probably even laugh about Charlie throwing up at Disney World because she sat next to him at the ice cream parlor, and some of it splashed onto her sneakers.

When someone answers, I almost expect to hear Nikki's voice, so I'm surprised at the sound of Dad's deep voice.

"Hi, Dad," I say. "It's Olivia." Charlie pokes me. "And Charlie."

"Hey, Butter Bean," he says, sweet as cotton candy, and I want to cry with relief that he's being nice.

Charlie pulls on my elbow. "Can I talk to him now, Livi?"

I push Charlie's hand away and give him the stink eye. I already told him I needed to ask Dad something.

"Liviiiii," he whines.

I cover the phone. "Not yet, Charlie."

He sticks out his tongue, and I turn my back to him.

"Dad?" I ask. "Still there?"

"Yes," he says, suddenly donning his impatient voice. "But I've got to get to the track soon so . . . Oh, crap. I forgot to call you guys yesterday, didn't I?"

"Yes," I say quietly, not wanting to make him feel worse than I'm sure he already does.

"Sorry, Butter Bean. Real sorry. Lots going on here and—"

"It's okay," I tell him.

"What's okay?" Charlie asks.

"Shhh," I say, and hunch forward for more privacy. I

feel Charlie poke my back with the tips of his skinny fingers, but I ignore him.

"Butter Bean," Dad says. "I'm sorry to rush you, but I really need to—"

"Dad, there's a chance for me to be on *Jeopardy!*"

"The *Jeopardy!?*"

"Yup. The one we watched together," I remind him.

"I know," he says. "Your old man hasn't lost his memory yet. That's great, baby. Let me know how it goes. Hon, put your brother on so I can get going now. Okay?"

I squeeze the phone, as though it will help me hang on to Dad a little longer. "But there's one thing." I need to hurry, but it's hard to ask him.

"Yes," he snaps. "Go on, Olivia."

My chest feels tight. "It's just that I need a parent to register me to take this test online, then I can—"

"Your mom can do that, Olivia. Put Charlie on. I've got to go." I picture Dad glancing at his watch with the blackjack cards on its face that Mom and I got him for his birthday about five years ago.

Charlie pulls the bottom of my shirt. "Now, Livi?"

I turn. Charlie's eyes are bright and wide, and I want to hand him the phone to make him happy, but I have to ask Dad about signing me up first.

"Dad, do you think maybe you could register me? It's really easy and—"

"Olivia," Dad says sharply. "That's the kind of stuff your mom does."

I look at the ceiling as though I have X-ray vision and can see Mom lying in bed. *Mom can't sign me up right now.* "But, Dad . . ." And I realize I sound as whiny as Charlie, but I don't know what else to do. *Why can't he understand?* "It won't take long. I promise." My voice gets high and tight. "You just have to—"

"I don't just have to do anything . . . except get to this first race on time. There's a long shot I want to bet on." Dad lets out a rush of air. "I'm sure your mom will be happy to take care of this. Now put Charlie on."

My throat tightens. "But, Dad—"

"Never mind," he says. "I've got to go."

"But—"

"Damn it!"

Why is Dad acting like this? Sometimes he'll talk to me for a long time. Once, we chatted about a book he was reading—*Outliers*—for almost half an hour. It explored the hidden reasons behind ubersuccessful people. Dad had said the author explained that people need to practice something for ten thousand hours before they can be truly great at it. I remember wondering if I'd studied trivia for ten thousand hours.

But right now, the anger in Dad's voice scares me.

"Look, Olivia, tell Charlie I'll call later."

Click.

"Now, Livi?" Charlie asks, holding out his palm.

I put the phone in Charlie's hand, the sound of the dial tone already oozing from the speaker, and run up to my room before I start crying.

Are We in Jeopardy?

I lie on my bed with the butterfly comforter pulled to my chin and stare at the bright yellow ceiling, wishing it were painted a depressing shade of gray to match my mood. *Why can't Dad do this one thing for me?* It's not like I ask him for much. And why couldn't he wait a few more seconds to talk with Charlie? How is Charlie supposed to understand that Dad would rather go to the racetrack than talk to him? No wonder Mom used to get so upset with Dad.

Mom!

I pull the comforter over my head. In the stifling darkness, I think of horrible diseases Mom might have: ovarian cancer, Lou Gehrig's disease or trichotillomania, which is the compulsive need to pull one's hair out, strand by strand. Tears trickle down my cheeks, and

I wipe my leaky nose on my comforter. I picture Mom handing me a tissue and telling me I'm being gross, which only makes me cry harder.

I need my mom!

I'm sniffing and sobbing and making it so stuffy under my comforter that I fling it off me.

Mom is standing there. Her hair is flat and greasy. Her eyes are pink and puffy, like Charlie said.

"Mom?"

"Olivia?"

Mom's voice sounds hoarse, and I get scared all over again that something terrible is wrong with her.

"Why are you crying?" Mom asks. "What's wrong?"

Everything! "Nothing." But I start blubbering again. My shoulders heave in spasms, and I have to take my glasses off to swipe at my leaking eyes.

Mom climbs into bed next to me. She grabs Phil around the neck and scoots close to me. The warmth from her body makes me feel better.

"Now, tell me what's wrong," Mom says.

"What's wrong with you?"

Mom lets out a breath. "I'm sorry, Olivia." She kisses the top of my head. "I know I haven't been myself since Tuesday night, but that's over now."

"What happened?" I remember Mom and Neil's talk Tuesday, him telling her everything's going to be okay.

"Oh, Livi," Mom says. "After twenty-four years of loyalty to that newspaper, they laid me off."

My eyes go wide. "They laid you off from the newspaper? But how . . . ?"

"It'll be okay," Mom says, touching her head to mine. "I'll find another job."

"Yes, but . . . you've worked there for, like, forever. You have your own column."

"I know," Mom says, sniffing. "That's what hurts. But I'll find something else."

"Why did they . . . I mean, did you do something wrong?"

Mom shakes her head. "Money, Livi. They haven't been making much money, so they've been laying people off."

"Because they can't afford to pay them?"

"Yes. I guess I thought I would . . . I don't know." Mom's quiet, but then she looks up and kisses me on the head. "But don't you worry. Like I said, I'll find something else."

"Sure you will," I say, relieved Mom doesn't have some horrible disease that makes her want to pull her hair out strand by strand. "You're amazing."

"Thanks, Livi." Mom puts her arm around my shoulders and squeezes. "We'll need to be extra careful, though, until I find something else."

"Careful?"

"You know," Mom says. "Cut back on things to save money."

"Oh, I know. I'll get my trivia books from the library instead of the bookstore. And you don't have to treat me to lunch at school on Fridays anymore. I'll bring a peanut butter and jelly sandwich from home."

For some reason, this makes Mom's eyes swell with tears, and she gives me a bone-crunching squeeze. "Olivia, you're the best. What would I do without you?"

I shrug, but inside I feel good, like I'm part of a team. I feel like I did when Mom depended on me after Dad left.

Dad.

I've got to figure out a way to visit him, like getting on *Jeopardy!*, to remind him of all the fun we have when we're together. Being far away from him isn't good. It's like he forgets how much he loves me and Charlie. And I bet there's no way Mom could afford plane tickets to California now.

If I passed the online test and the tryouts and got on *Jeopardy!*, not only would I get to see Dad, I could win us a lot of money. That might really help now.

"Mom, there's this—" I bite my bottom lip. As much as I want to ask her, need to ask her, one look at Mom's haggard face tells me this is not the right time to mention

Kids Week. Besides, if I make it to the tryouts, it will require a trip to Washington, DC, for a test and interview, and that would cost extra money we probably don't have.

I slump.

"What, Livi?" Mom asks, leaning into me.

Being part of a team means looking out for your teammates. And right now, my teammate has pink, puffy eyes and tear-stained cheeks.

"Nothing," I say. "How about if I go make dinner?"

"That would be great," Mom says. "Let me take a quick shower and I'll come down and help."

"Okay," I say, glad to have my mom back. I just wish she hadn't lost her job. I hate to see her upset. And I wish I could ask her about registering me for the *Jeopardy!* test now. But I'm sure things will get better and I'll ask her soon.

Downstairs, Charlie's sitting at his place at the table, smashing two racing cars together.

I ruffle his hair and give him a Pop-Tart before starting dinner.

What's in the Red Envelope?

When I trudge down to breakfast the next morning, no one's there, but there's an envelope at my place at the table—a red envelope with a note on top:

> *Olivia, I've taken Charlie to the bus so your mother could sleep in. This is for you, Brainy Bean.*

Brainy Bean? What does that mean? Is Neil making fun of me?

I run my finger over the envelope. My name is printed in neat block letters: OLIVIA BEAN. The envelope appears to hold a birthday card or a Valentine's Day card, but it's not either of those days. I pry open the flap.

Inside is a greeting card. On the front of the card are

giant bubble letters that say "Good luck!" And inside, it says "You deserve it!" Underneath, Neil signed his first name. Just his name. Not *Love, Neil*. Or *Like, Neil*. Or *Your friend, Neil*. Just *Neil*.

And I don't get it . . . until I unfold the white paper tucked inside the card. My lips move as I read. And now I get it . . . and can't believe it.

My hands shake as I read the words.

It's the registration confirmation to take the online test to try out for Kids Week. It tells me the date and time of the test, instructions and the password Neil chose for me: *Brainy Bean*.

Neil did this for me even though I haven't been the nicest person to him lately. Um, ever. Translation: I've thought of him as barely higher on the evolutionary scale than a sea monkey. But now, Neil's somewhere up there with Ken Jennings—one of *Jeopardy!*'s all-time biggest winners and my personal hero.

I'll never forget what Neil did for me no matter how old I get, unless I get Alzheimer's disease like Grandpa Jack had, but then it won't be my fault.

Double Jeopardy! Round

What's the Worst Way to Save Money?

I can't eat. I try, but I can't. Neil made a pot of his world-famous vegetarian stew to give me energy for the big night. He even cooked biscuits on top—my favorite. After fifteen minutes of tapping my foot under the table and reviewing inane trivia in my mind—*James Buchanan was the only U.S. president who never married*—I manage to swallow one carrot. One carrot! And even that barely slides down my throat.

"Olivia," Neil says. "You have to eat something more than a slice of carrot. Your brain needs energy to work."

"I'll be okay," I say, feeling totally wired and excited. "I don't want to throw up."

"Too much information," Mom says. "*We're* eating, even if you're not."

"Throwing up is okay," Charlie says. "Emetomaniacs feel like they're going to throw up all the time."

"We know," Mom and I say to Charlie at the same time.

"Okay," he says. "You don't have to yell."

"Sorry," Mom says. "I think we're all a little excited for Livi."

Neil nods at me and says, "That we are, Brainy Bean."

I blush and look down. It's because of Neil that I'm able to take the test tonight. It's because of him that I have a chance to get on *Jeopardy!*

"How long is this test?" Mom asks.

"Test. West. Fest. Nest," Charlie sings while poking at his bowl of stew.

"Give it a *rest*," Neil says.

"Lest. Best. Test. Test. *Test!*"

"Pest," I mutter.

"Heard that," Charlie says.

Mom nudges me. "How long?"

"Oh, the test is exactly ten minutes. I have to answer thirty questions in that time." I swallow a bite of biscuit, then check my watch. "Aaaah!" I push back from the table and sprint toward the stairs. "Test starts in twenty," I yell. "Got to log in early."

I hear Mom drop her spoon and say something, but

don't have time to process. I've got to get on Mom's computer and log in. *Brainy Bean is ready for action!*

While I'm tapping my socked foot, waiting for the computer to connect, Mom bursts into the room. "Get your shoes on."

"Huh?" I say, and check the computer screen again. "Mom, the computer won't connect to the Internet."

"Olivia," Mom shrieks, her face turning red. "Get your shoes on. Neil's taking you to the library. Hurry!"

"What?" I have no idea what she's talking about. "I can't go to the library now. The test starts in eighteen minutes!" I tap the screen to show her, but I notice it still hasn't connected. "Mom?"

Neil skids into the bedroom, shaking his keys. "Ready? Let's go. I think we'll make it."

I rise. *Is the computer broken? How will I take the test? "Mom!"*

She grabs my shoulders and looks into my eyes. "Livi, I'm so sorry. Yesterday, I had the Internet service turned off to save money. We were paying fifty-nine dollars a month for it. I completely . . . with everything going on . . . I . . . forgot about the test."

"Oh, my . . ." I sink onto Mom's bed. "How . . ." My face is in my hands. My shoulders bob.

"Olivia!" Neil says in a strong voice. "Get up. I can

get you to the library in fifteen minutes, but we need to hurry."

I shake my head in my hands. "No. No."

"I'll set you up in my office in the back," Neil says. "But we've got to leave now."

I glance up; Neil is windmilling his right arm, like he's signaling a runner to go to home base. "Now, Olivia. Now."

I stand and shuffle a few steps, like I'm walking through deep water.

"Now, Livi. Now." Charlie windmills both arms and jumps, like this is the most exciting day ever.

But it's not. It's the worst day ever, because I know that even if Neil drives fast, we can't get to the library in less than twenty minutes. Then we'd still have to get me set up on a computer. And the most important test in the world starts in fifteen minutes.

I stop moving. "We won't make it."

"We've got to try," Neil says, but I can tell by the look on his face he knows it's hopeless, too.

I trudge from the room, trailed by Mom's voice; "I'm so sorry."

I drag myself across the hall into my room. My body feels like it's made of lead—atomic number 82, symbol Pb. It takes all my strength to heave myself onto my bed. Except it turns out, I have enough energy left to hurl Phil at the far wall and say a word I'd heard Dad use once, when he lost during a poker game at our house.

I burrow under the butterfly comforter and let out a long breath.

Game over.

Knock, Knock. Who's There?

I'm buried under my comforter for only a minute when the most unpleasant thought comes to mind.

I bound out of bed and don't bother with sneakers. I thunder down the stairs and out the front door, hoping no one follows. I don't have time to explain.

The concrete is cold through my socks as I bob from foot to foot in front of Tucker Thomas's door. I ring the bell and look around, hoping no one sees me. I don't want to associate myself with Tucker. When will that boy grow up and stop calling me Olivia Bean, Hula Hoop Queen? It's been two years since the unfortunate hula hoop incident! And the note he slipped into my hand really irritated me. What did he mean by *makes your face look mean?*

I thought Tucker Thomas was a fun kid to hang out with when we were younger, but now? He's totally and completely immature.

Still . . .

I ring the bell again and glance at my watch. The test begins in twelve minutes, and I can't let it start without me.

Mr. Thomas's silver Fit is parked on the street and there are lights on inside the house, so I know they're home. I take a deep breath and realize I'd rather have my head smashed between two thick trivia books than ask Tucker Thomas for something. But I have no choice. I bang on the door as hard as I can.

The door flies open. "Bean? You don't have to bang down the door."

The sight of Tucker makes me want to run home and hide under my comforter again. A tornado has ravaged his hair, a purple stain graces his T-shirt and he's chomping on a piece of celery like a cow chewing cud. I shiver. "I rang the doorbell, but—"

"Doorbell's broken, Bean," Tucker says, and closes the door.

He closed the door in my face!

At first, I think it's a joke and wait for him to open it. I check my watch and bob from foot to frozen foot, thinking about how much I dislike Tucker Thomas. If only there were another way. But there isn't, so I stab the doorbell several times before remembering it's broken. Then I pound on the door.

Hurry!

The door opens again, and Tucker stands with his head tilted. "What?"

You're a jerk! Through chattering teeth, I say, "I have . . . to use . . . your computer."

"Huh?"

"Your computer. I have nine minutes before the online *Jeopardy!* test starts."

"Oh," he says. "You mean the test I told you about?"

I'm so glad he gets it. "Yes! Now, please let me in."

Tucker opens the door wider, then blocks the way with his body. "Why should I let you in, Bean? You've been a jerk to me lately. Ever since I gave you that note, you've been . . . you've been . . . And I know you tripped me in the cafeteria."

"I didn't!" I say indignantly.

"You did!" He stands with his arms crossed over the stain on his shirt. "Even Matt said so. He saw you."

"Matt's an idiot."

"Well, yeah, but still . . ."

"Look, Tucker, if I tripped you, it was an accident." I

134

bite my lower lip and force two words out of my mouth. "I'm sorry."

"It wasn't an accident, Bean," Tucker says.

He's right. It wasn't. I was angry about the note and I tripped him on purpose. His open carton of chocolate milk went flying and made a huge mess. "Look, Tucker," I say, desperate to get inside before it's too late. "I said I'm sorry. And I am sorry!" My lips feel frozen. "I don't know what more you want."

"Why are you acting this way, Bean? I've been nice to you and you've been a jerk!"

Me? I want to shout, *You, Tucker Thomas, have been the jerk!* But I hold it in because using Tucker's computer is my only chance.

"Besides," he says, gnawing on the celery stick, "why can't you use your own computer?"

I shake from the frigid air and from frustration. *Tucker Thomas, let me in! I've got about eight minutes until the most important test in the world starts.* I force myself to speak slowly. "My mom lost—" I snap my mouth shut. I can't believe I almost told him. I don't care how much I need to use his computer, I'm not telling Tucker Thomas that Mom canceled the Internet to save money. I'm not telling him that even with Neil's income, we've cut back on *everything*, like switching to generic toilet paper that feels like sandpaper on my butt. And I'm not telling him that I'm eligible now for free lunches at school. Those things are none of his business.

I cross my arms, partly because I'm cold and partly because I'm mad.

He uncrosses his. "How come you only come over when you want something, Bean?"

I swallow hard and say, "Tucker, please." I feel humiliated having to beg him to let me into his house. "Please!"

Tucker laughs and a piece of chewed-up celery flies out of his mouth. "It's too late to make up, Bean. I tried to be nice to you and you've been . . . you've been—"

"*Nice?*" I scream outside in the dark night, while the bottoms of my feet are so cold they feel like frozen fish filets. "You call me Olivia Bean, Hula Hoop Queen!"

"So?" Tucker says.

"So?" I whisper/shout, thinking of going back into my house. Getting on *Jeopardy!* is not worth dealing with Tucker Thomas. "I hate being called that!"

Tucker reels back. "Why didn't you say so, Bean? Everyone calls you that."

"Everyone *used* to call me that," I correct. "No one does anymore. Except you and Matt. And I hate it! Now, can I please come in and use your computer for ten measly minutes?" I check my watch and see I still have six minutes before my dream disappears. I can't stand myself for doing it, but I put my hands together in the begging position and say, "This is so important. Please, Tucker."

"Nah," Tucker says, and shuts the door.

"Tucker!" I scream at the closed door. "I hate your vile, slimy, putrid—"

The door swings open. Mrs. Thomas stands there, arms crossed. "What's going on?" she asks, leveling Tucker with one of those parent stares.

"It's just Bean," Tucker says, and starts to walk upstairs.

"Well, let her in." Mrs. Thomas opens the door for me. "Olivia, I'm sorry Tucker was rude." She glances at my socked feet when I walk in, and I wish I'd worn sneakers.

I want to be polite and have a conversation with Mrs. Thomas, because she's really nice and I haven't spoken with her much since Tucker and I became enemies. But I have four minutes before the test starts. Four precious minutes. "Mrs. Thomas, I'm sorry to barge in but—"

"That's okay, Olivia. It's nice to see you. You know you're welcome here any time. Can I get you—"

"I'm having a *Jeopardy!* emergency here!" I practically shout. I know I sound like a lunatic, but I don't care. "I need to get on a computer in the next four minutes and take this very important test." I can't believe

I'm talking this fast. "But my mom—" I can't say the next part, so I tell a little lie. "Our computer isn't working right now. So—"

Mrs. Thomas nods, grabs my arm and nudges me toward the stairs. "Go, Olivia. Use the computer in Tucker's room." She yells upstairs, "Tucker Thomas, let Olivia use your computer right now or I swear, I'll take it out of your room for a month! Do you hear me?"

I hear her. She's shouting next to my ear.

"Whatever!" Tucker screams, and I let out the breath I've been holding.

"Thank you!" I charge up the stairs, noticing new photos on the wall along the staircase. Updated photos of Tucker—less-cute ones!

It's been a long time since I was in Tucker's room, but I can see it's as messy as ever. That boy probably hasn't hung up a piece of clothing since the Phillies won the World Series.

I motor through stinky piles of socks, jeans and underwear—*ew!*—and plop onto his computer chair, tapping my feet on the floor to get them warm. I wonder how long it takes for frostbite to set in and hope that particular question isn't on the test.

The test!

Tucker is lying on his bed, hands behind his head, watching me. There's a giant map on the wall beside him that I don't remember from before. No wonder that boy is so good at geography.

But that's not important now. Frostbite isn't important now. Nothing is important except getting online.

On Tucker's computer, I type fast, get on the website and sign in with the password Neil picked for me—*Brainy Bean*.

Tucker taps the wall, annoying me.

On the left side of the screen, there's a photo of Alex Trebek, looking dapper in his pin-striped suit. On the right side is a clock. And even though it's exactly eight o'clock, the timer says there are five minutes before the test begins. *What's up with that?* I watch the time tick down and then I get it. The test will begin five minutes after eight, I guess, to give kids a chance to get to their computers. *Good thinking, Alex. Extra time is a good thing.*

I let out a big breath.

I made it!

What Do More Than
Ten Thousand Kids Have in Common?

Even though I'm ready—I've spent practically my entire life preparing—when the first category and answer appear on the screen ("Bodies of Water: This Great Lake borders Ohio and Pennsylvania"), I'm surprised.

It's really happening.

I crack my neck from side to side, wiggle my fingers and remind myself:

> *Take the full twenty seconds with each one.*
> *There's no advantage to answering early.*
> *Don't answer in the form of a question.*
> *Try to spell correctly.*

"Lake Erie!" Tucker blurts out from behind me.

"Tucker!" I hadn't realized he'd gotten off his bed and

was peering over my shoulder. "You can't help!" But I type in "Lake Erie" because I knew that one anyway.

After twenty seconds, a bell dings and a new category and answer appear.

"Name the Poet: 'Two roads diverged in a wood, and I—I took the one less traveled by, and that has made all the difference.'"

I know this one, so I take a moment to glance at Tucker. He's leaning forward, practically resting his chin on my shoulder, but at least his lips are pressed together and he's not blurting out any information.

I type "Robert Frost" and wait until I hear the ding and the program captures my answer.

"Children's Authors: This man wrote a novel about 'some pig.'"

I know this one. Of course I know it. Mom read this book to me twice when I was younger. And I read it once by myself and cried. So, why is my brain refusing to cooperate? My big, beautiful brain is totally constipated. *Bad timing, big, beautiful brain!*

This, I know, is what separates the winners from the losers on *Jeopardy!* All contestants know tons of information or they couldn't make it onto the show, but their ability to bring that information quickly to the surface is what helps them win.

Pig. Spider. Come on. I feel Tucker's breath on my

neck. It tickles, and I'm about to yell at him when the answer comes to me. I type "E. B. White." Then my brain surprises me with a bonus—"Elwyn Brooks White." I manage to type his full name before the computer dings and captures my answer.

"Score!" Tucker shouts and bops me on the head.

"Hey!"

"Sorry."

I feel him step back and am glad.

"Texting Acronyms: TTYL."

"Easy," Tucker mutters.

I type "Talk to you later" and say, "Tucker, quiet!"

"Sorry."

"Really, stop. You could have taken the test if you'd wanted to."

"I didn't want to." He flops back onto his bed.

The next question is: "Measurement: Three of these make up a yard."

"Foot," I type, then change it to "Feet" and realize mine are finally warm.

I stumble on a Biology question and completely blow a U.S. Cities question. *Blasted geography!*

Before I realize it, the *Jeopardy!* "Think Music" plays and this message appears on the screen: "You will NOT be notified of your score. Parents of applicants who are

selected to attend our in-person audition will be con-
tacted by the *Jeopardy!* Contestant Department."

It's over.

I inhale deeply, which is a bad idea, because all the
dirty clothes in Tucker's room make it smell like the
monkey house at the zoo.

"You missed the U.S. Cities question."

"I know, Tucker."

"It was Austin. Austin, Texas."

"Oh."

"You can use my atlas to study, if you want."

"Thanks," I say, "but the test is over."

"What about the next part? Don't you have to study
for that?"

"If I make it," I say.

"You'll make it, Bean."

I reel back. "Um, thanks, Tucker."

"No sweat." Tucker nods. "Now get out. I have homework to do." He roots through piles of papers on his desk.
"If I can find it."

Now, that's the Tucker I know.

As I make my way through dirty-laundry land mines
toward the door, I see Tucker's hamster cage on his bureau
and walk over. But there's only one hamster inside. I look
at Tucker.

"Gypsy," he says. "About a year ago."

"I'm so sorry." I tap softly on the plastic water bottle to say hello to Rose.

"You still got DJ?" Tucker asks.

"Oh, yeah. He still meows in the middle of the night and climbs onto my head when I'm sleeping."

Tucker smiles. "That's good. See you later, Bean."

"Later," I say, making my way down the stairs, past the photos of Tucker along the wall and outside onto the cold, cold landing in front of our homes.

As soon as I'm inside our house, Mom and Neil rush out from the kitchen.

"Where'd you go?" Mom asks.

"Tucker's," I say, thinking of Gypsy being gone and how I didn't even know about it. Tucker must have been crushed, and I wasn't even there for him. *Maybe I have been kind of mean.*

"Good thinking," Neil says.

I realize he's talking about me using Tucker's computer to take the test.

"How'd it go?" Neil asks.

Normally, I'd give Neil a snarky answer or ignore him. Not today. Not anymore. "I think it went well." I remember typing in "Elwyn Brooks White" at the last second. "Really well, actually. But I'm pretty sure I missed two. Maybe only one, though."

"That sounds fantastic to me," Neil says.

"Me too," comes a tiny voice from the top of the stairs.

"Go to bed, Charlie," Mom says.

Charlie bends and talks through the slats in the banister. "Livi, did you know it takes a mommy rat three weeks to make a baby rat?"

"Charlie," Mom says in a threatening tone.

"I'm going," Charlie says, and disappears. "And some rats can go longer without water than camels!" he shouts.

Mom shakes her head, then looks at me and clasps her hands together. "I'm so proud of you, Jelly Bean."

The nickname throws me because it's Dad who calls me cute nicknames, although he hasn't lately.

"When do you find out if you made it to the auditions?" Neil asks.

I peel my socks off, lean on the wall and rub each foot. "I read on a message board that someone from the *Jeopardy!* staff will call if I made it. If not, I'll never hear anything." I think of the year that happened, and how hard it was.

"You'll make it," Neil says.

"You'll make it," Charlie shouts from his bedroom.

"Charlie!" Mom yells.

"I'm in bed."

"And be quiet," Mom calls.

"*I am being quiet!*" he screams.

Mom sighs.

Neil shakes his head, but smiles.

Neil's beginning to grow on me, and not in the way mold grows on a shower curtain.

"So we have to wait for a call?" Neil asks.

I like that he said *we*. "Yup. I read on the message board that more than ten thousand kids take the online test, but only five hundred are invited to the audition. Only five hundred! If I'm one of the five hundred, I'll get a call."

"Yowza," Neil says. "Tough odds."

"Indeed," Mom says. "Hey, speaking of phone calls, your father called while you were at Tucker's. He wants you to call him back."

"Dad called?" I'm stunned.

It's not even Wednesday.

How Can Olivia Afford a Trip to California and Normal Toilet Paper?

Dad picks up on the first ring, like he was waiting for me to call. "Hey, Beany Baby."

"Hi, Dad." I slide down the wall and hunch to keep the call private.

"What's up?"

"I took the online test for *Jeopardy!*" When I say this, my stomach knots because I remember he wouldn't sign me up.

"Marion—er, your mother told me. That's great."

But his voice doesn't sound like it's great. His voice sounds small and sad.

"Think you'll make it?" he asks.

I shrug, worried about how Dad's voice sounds. "Dad, are you okay?"

"Oh, yeah," he says way too fast. "Your old man's fine. Just fine. Never better." Then he laughs a fake laugh that tells me he's not fine at all. I wonder if I should tell Mom.

I chew on a thumbnail.

"Lovely Livi?" he says, his voice slurring a bit. "You still there?"

"I'm here." I curl tighter, my lower back pressed against the wall.

"So how did you do on that *Jeopardy!* test?"

"I guess good, but—"

"Well. You did well, Livi," Dad says. "How could you do anything but well? You've got Bean genes. Right?"

I think of my deficiency in geography. That's not from Bean genes. It's just my own personal problem.

"Hey, Livi?"

"Yes?"

"I was telling your mom how much I want you to visit."

My heart does a little thump; then I realize Dad didn't say he wants Charlie to visit. It would be fun to have Dad to myself, but . . . "What about Charlie?" I ask.

"Of course," Dad slurs. "You and Charlie. Charlie and you. Didn't I say that, Jelly Bean?"

"Um, no." Dad's voice sounds strange.

"Stella would *love* to have you both here." Dad

stretches out the word "love" like it has thirteen syllables.

I cringe at the thought of Stella, all spiky heels and big hair.

"Maybe we'll play Skee-Ball together at the pier. Would you like that?"

Dad and I haven't played Skee-Ball since I was six, but I say, "Sure."

"And we can get soft serve. Chocolate and vanilla swirl. Your favorite. See, Jelly Bean? I remembered."

Actually, chocolate and vanilla swirl is Mom's favorite. Charlie and I like vanilla custard with rainbow sprinkles.

"Hey," I whisper. "Maybe we could watch *Jeopardy!* together."

"Like we used to," he says.

This makes me feel like crying. "Yeah." I sniff. "Like we used to."

"There's one problem, though, Jelly Bean," Dad says, slurring the word "problem."

Is Dad okay?

"Things aren't going so great at the moment, and I was hoping your mom would be able to . . ."

Dad doesn't finish the sentence. My heart sinks. I know there's no way Mom can pay for plane tickets to California. We can't even afford normal toilet paper!

"But don't worry," Dad says, and suddenly I'm hopeful because I know he has a plan. He always has a plan. "I'll hit the big one," he says. "One of these days, Jelly Bean, I'll hit a jackpot and bring you and Charlie here in style. A limo ride all the way across the country. Would you like that?"

"Sure," I whisper, holding back tears, because I know Dad will never hit "the big one." And even if he did, it wouldn't change the things that matter. He'd still live all the way across the country with Stella the Stealer and my former best friend.

"Livi?" Dad asks in a quiet voice.

"Mm-hmm?"

"I miss you, baby girl." Then Dad makes a choking sound and hangs up.

"Dad?" I lean forward. "You still there? Dad!" But I'm talking to a dial tone. I squeeze the phone to my heart and whisper, "I miss you, too."

Did They Call?

Waiting is terrible.

When the phone rings, I jump, but it's never for me. Except when Dad calls on Wednesday nights. *When he remembers.* On those nights, I hope Nikki starts talking to me again, because it's hard not having a best friend to talk with, especially when it comes to waiting for *Jeopardy!* to call.

I try talking to Julia, Carly and Brooke about it at lunch, but all they want to talk about is their stupid trip to Bolivia, what they'll wear and if there will be cute boys there. When I brought up *Jeopardy!* again the other day, Julia said, "Blah, blah, blah. *Jeopardy!* We get it, Olivia. You want to get on the show. Stop talking about it already."

I stopped talking. And now I spend lunch period wondering why I even sit with them.

Mom still hasn't found a job. Every time there's a bill in the mail, she winces, like a dentist is drilling in her mouth and hit a nerve. And every day after school, Mom anticipates my question—"Did they call?"—and shakes her head.

I have this recurring nightmare that Mom cancels our phone service to save money, and the *Jeopardy!* people try to call but can't get through.

Even Tucker's been asking if I've heard anything. I finally had to tell him to stop bugging me, because it's been a month since I took the test.

When I'm in bed at night, I hear Neil come home from work and ask Mom, "Anything yet?"

I picture Mom shaking her head, and I feel like a loser. A failure. A kid whose head is stuffed with useless knowledge. *The number for pi is 3.14. There are 366 days in a leap year. Victoria Woodhull was the first woman to run for president of the United States, 50 years before women were allowed to vote. There are 64 squares on a checkerboard.*

Please call!

Charlie's the only one who doesn't bother me about it. He's too busy smashing racing cars into each other, annoying DJ and spouting gross trivia. *Livi, did you know bats have thumbs? Livi, female hamsters smell worse than male hamsters. Livi, fingernails grow faster than toenails. Livi . . .*

With each passing day, I'm more convinced I've blown it. I must have missed more than two questions. I must have misspelled some things. Done something wrong. *But what?* Maybe there are just too many smart kids who took the test, and I'm not going to get chosen. Me, Olivia Bean—the girl who needs this more than anyone else possibly could.

Did my geography deficiency somehow show up on the test? I'm positive I didn't miss more than one geography question. And I've actually been improving in that area. I got a C on that first geography test in school, but solid Bs on the two tests since. Even Tucker gave me a thumbs-up when we got our most recent test back.

And Mom hung it on the refrigerator door.

If I got on *Jeopardy!*, I could show Dad how much I've improved at geography, even though I still can't remember some of the basic stuff. I wonder if Dad still watches *Jeopardy!* And if he does, does he watch it with Nikki?

Thinking about this makes my stomach clench. I bend forward and try to think about something else, like if those *Jeopardy!* people will ever call. But that doesn't help my stomach feel better.

Last night, I overheard Mom and Neil whisper-talking.

She said we're running through our savings faster than she'd expected. He told her not to worry. She said there's not enough money for Christmas presents this year. He said he'd find a second job.

After that, no one said anything, but Mom cried softly. I wanted to run downstairs and hug her, tell her I'd figure out a way to help, but somehow I knew Neil was holding her and she'd be okay.

If I'm lucky enough to get on *Jeopardy!* and win, I'll take all of us to Disney World; then I'll give the rest of the money to Mom so that she can stop worrying.

Oh, please call!

What Do Wreaths Have to Do with Anything?

It's unusually cold for the first week of December. On my way home from school, I pull my collar up against my neck and walk fast, but when I arrive, the tips of my ears and nose still feel frozen.

Tucker usually walks home with me now, but he stayed after school today for debate club. He's such a nerd!

I let myself into our house and am overwhelmed by the fresh scent of pine.

"Hi," Mom calls from her chair across the living room. Wreaths are piled all over, and one is on Mom's lap. She's threading a sparkly gold ribbon through it.

I drop my backpack. "What are you doing? And why does our house smell like a pine forest?"

"Mmm." Mom inhales deeply. "Don't these smell good, Livi?" She's smiling.

"Yes, but—"

"Ms. Duxbury, down the street, decorates wreaths for the holidays. People pay a lot of money for these things." Mom holds up the wreath with the gold ribbon threaded partway through it. "I don't get the appeal. But, whatever."

I make my way through the piles of wreaths to get to Mom and sit on the stool in front of her.

Mom is smiling so broadly the skin beside her eyes crinkles. "Ms. Duxbury had more orders than she could handle—thank goodness!—so she threw some work my way and taught me how to do it. Wasn't that nice of her?"

"I guess." Really, I can't believe Mom's decorating wreaths. When it comes to crafts, she's the anti–Martha Stewart. Mom shudders at the thought of sewing a tear in our Halloween costumes. Getting near a hot glue gun probably frightens her more than a real gun. "But, um, wreaths? Really?"

She shrugs. "I'm just going to make these for the holidays so we'll have some extra moolah." Mom's eyes go wide and she rubs her palms together. "We could really use the money *now*."

Why the emphasis on "now"? Panic swells in my chest. "Have we run out of money already?"

"Oh, no," Mom says, shaking her head and looking way too happy. "Being careful has really helped. And Neil's going to work a couple shifts at the Stop and Shop till I find another job. We're fine."

"Mom?"

"Hmm?" Mom threads gold ribbon through the wreath, her hands trembling.

"Why are you smiling so much?"

"Am I?"

"Yes! You haven't stopped smiling since I got home, and it's freaking me out. No offense, Mom, but you're usually not this happy. Especially about wreaths!" Then a thought begins to bubble, and I smile, too. Maybe the extra money from the wreaths will pay for plane tickets for me and Charlie to visit Dad at Christmas.

"Well," Mom says, finally putting down the wreath. "I thought we'd need a little extra cash for, I don't know, maybe a special trip somewhere."

"California?" I practically lunge at her.

"No, why?" Her shoulders slump. "Do you want to visit your father?"

I shake my head, even though I do want to visit him.

"I'm talking about Washington, DC." Mom tilts her head, like she expects me to read her mind.

"DC?" *Is this something about geography I should understand but don't?*

157

Mom grabs my shoulders, and is so close to my face that I can smell the peanut butter on her breath. "They called, Livi."

I stop breathing.

Mom nods, still gripping my shoulders. "They called. They *called.*"

"Auditions are in DC," I say, swallowing hard.

Mom nods so vigorously, I think her head will pop off and topple onto the wreaths on the floor.

I need to ask again to be sure. "The *Jeopardy!* people called?"

"Yes."

"And I made it to the audition round? Me?" I touch my chest. "Olivia Bean?"

"Yes," Mom says again, laughing. She takes my cheeks in her warm, pine-scented palms. "Yes, you, Olivia Bean."

Mom barely sneaks a kiss onto my forehead before I spring up. "*Yes!*"

We shove a few wreaths out of the way with our feet so that we can hug each other and jump around.

"I made it!"

"You made it!"

"You made it, Livi. You made it!" Charlie bounds down the stairs, zigzagging through wreaths, and tackles my legs. He's got my thighs in a death grip of happiness. "Made what, Livi?"

Mom and I crack up. "Your sister made it to the *Jeopardy!* auditions."

Charlie squeezes my legs. "I told you you'd make it!"

"Indeed you did, little man," I say.

We hang on to each other and jump and jump until we stumble and fall breathless onto a pile of wreaths, laughing and crying all at the same time.

And weirdly enough, the only thing that keeps this moment from being 100 percent perfect is that I wish Neil were here, celebrating with us.

What Is "I Don't Know What"?

Even though Mom gave up getting her hair colored at "the shop" to save money and we've been eating an awful lot of rice, beans and frozen veggies lately, she bought me a brand-new skirt, blouse and shoes, and let me have *my* hair done at "the shop."

Mom says that how I look and act is as important as how much I know. "You'll be judged not only on your ability to answer questions, Olivia, but also on your ability to be bright and friendly and have that certain *je ne sais quoi*," which I learned is a French expression that means "I don't know what."

I'm not sure what the judges will look for, but I'm glad Mom bought me new clothes. They're really nice. And my hair doesn't look flat and boring anymore.

If I pass the audition and get on the show, I'll finally

meet Alex Trebek. I can't wait to shake his hand and tell him how much I love the show, how I've been watching since I was little. And I'll have a chance to win money. Big money. Thousands and thousands of dollars that I know we can use now. I overheard Mom talking to her friend on the phone yesterday. She said, "Even with Neil's extra job at the Stop and Shop, things will still be extremely tight."

I have to get on that show. And I have to win!

I believe I have a chance, as long as . . .

As long as I don't freeze. That would ruin everything. I remember the unfortunate hula hoop incident in fifth grade and hope something like that doesn't happen.

I can't get this far only to have that happen to me . . . again.

What's Not Under the Christmas Tree?

Christmas morning, Charlie wakes us at 5:37. It feels like it's still the middle of the night. Even DJ is curled at the foot of my bed, one paw slung over his eyes, when I force myself out of bed and into the hall.

Charlie's wearing his red footie pajamas that are a little too tight. He hops from foot to foot like he needs to pee. "I waited as long as I could," he says.

"I'm sure you did," Mom says, her eyelids droopy.

We shuffle downstairs, and Neil goes into the kitchen to make coffee.

In the living room, I'm surprised to see so many gifts under the tree. With Mom out of work, I didn't expect to see more than maybe a couple small things for Charlie.

After Neil and Mom have a few sips of coffee and Charlie and I have orange juice, we open our gifts.

Charlie gets a book filled with gross facts about the human body. He opens to the middle and reads out loud. "'The human heart creates enough pressure to squirt blood thirty feet.' Thirty feet!" Charlie exclaims. "Isn't that cool?"

"Cool," Mom says, looking ashen.

"Open yours," Neil says.

I tear the paper from one of my gifts. It's a book containing tips about how to win on *Jeopardy!* from former champions. "Thank you." I hug the book to my chest.

"Use it well," Mom says.

"'Feet have five hundred thousand sweat glands and can produce more than a pint of sweat a day,'" Charlie says.

Mom wrinkles her nose.

Neil hands Charlie another gift. "Open this one."

The box brims with Matchbox cars.

Charlie's eyes go wide and he tosses the book aside to tear into the small packages of cars. It's thirty minutes before he opens the rest of his gifts—pajamas, underwear and socks. He keeps playing with the cars.

I get new pajamas and socks, too.

Mom and Neil give each other identical gifts—Scrabble sets.

"Great minds think alike," Mom says.

"We'll take mine back," Neil says. "I like the one you got better."

"They're exactly the same," Mom says, and they both crack up.

It's good to see Mom happy, even if Neil, not Dad, is the one making her feel that way.

Charlie hands each of us a picture he drew, and I wish I'd thought to make some kind of gift for everyone. But I've been too stressed about *Jeopardy!* All I did was make a batch of oatmeal raisin cookies for everyone to share, and even they were mostly burned.

Neil holds up his picture. It's a curved line with a bunch of dots under it. "It's a giant armpit," Charlie explains. "And those dots are the 516,000 bacteria crawling on it."

Neil nods. "This bad boy is going up on the fridge." And he takes the drawing into the kitchen.

Mom displays her picture of a smiling stick-figure lady surrounded by green rectangles.

"That's you," Charlie tells her. "Surrounded by all the money Livi wins when she gets on *Jeopardy!*"

Mom looks at me and smiles. "I love it!" she says. "Neil," she calls. "We've got another masterpiece to hang on the fridge."

Charlie puffs out his skinny chest as Mom carries his

drawing into the kitchen. "Do you like yours, Livi?" he asks.

I examine my drawing. It's a stick figure with a giant head, standing behind a big rectangle. The word *"Jeopardy!"* is spelled out across the top.

"That's you, Livi," Charlie says. "Winning on *Jeopardy!* Mom helped me with spelling."

I give my little bother a squeeze. But when I start to say something, I get choked up, so I walk to the kitchen to hang my drawing on the fridge too.

From the dining room, I see Mom and Neil with their faces mashed together. I back up a few steps and take a breath. I'm used to Neil living here now. I even like it sometimes. But I won't ever get used to seeing that!

I return to the living room.

"Aren't you going to hang my picture on the fridge?" Charlie asks.

"Later," I say, and open my new book.

"Now," Charlie says, snatching the drawing from my hand.

I reach out to stop him, but it's too late. He dashes toward the kitchen.

"Ewww!" Charlie screams. "You guys are gross!"

Mom and Neil crack up.

Charlie laughs too.

I don't. I stare at the unwrapped gifts under the tree and realize something is missing. There's nothing from Dad. He always sends us *something*. The first Christmas after Dad left, it was mittens that were a little too small for me and Charlie, but we wore them anyway. And last year, he sent toys that were too young for us, but at least he sent something.

Biting my bottom lip, I realize Dad probably bought something for Nikki this year.

I remember our last Christmas together before Dad left. There was no smooching in the kitchen that year. There was barely talking. I don't remember what I got that year, but I do remember Mom saying, "It's Christmas, Bill. You should be with your family."

"That's exactly why it's the best time to go," Dad said. "Hardly anyone will be there."

Mom turned her back then and Dad walked out. He drove to the casinos in Atlantic City.

Mom, Charlie and I had a quiet Christmas dinner by ourselves.

I don't want to think about that anymore, so I read my book of *Jeopardy!* tips.

At the end of the day, after Charlie's already asleep, Dad calls. "Merry Christmas, Butter Bean," he says, all excited. "Guess what Stella and I got each other for

Christmas?" Without waiting for my response, he blurts out, "A cruise. How crazy is that?"

"Crazy," I mutter. Then I bite my lip and say, "I guess Nikki will be going with you guys."

"Nah," Dad says. "She'll stay with a girlfriend or something."

A pain stabs my chest at the word "girlfriend." Of course Nikki has new friends. Why wouldn't she? She's really fun to hang out with.

"Oh," Dad says. "We got Nikki a purple iPod. She's had that thing plugged into her ears all day and—"

Then Dad's quiet, like he finally realizes he forgot to get anything for his own children. I expect him to tell me our gifts are on the way, but he doesn't. He clears his throat and doesn't even say he's sorry for forgetting us.

Out of sight, out of mind.

How Many Keys Are on a Piano?

"The drive to DC will take about three hours," Neil tells me. "Plenty of time to squeeze in more studying."

I nod, even though I already knew how long the drive would take and I don't plan to study more. My brain is filled to capacity. If I attempt to shoehorn even one new fact in, something important might fall out to make room.

Before we get in the car, Mom kisses Neil on the forehead and says, "Thanks for watching Charlie." Then she kneels in front of my little bother and says, "You be good, little man."

"I'll be awesome," Charlie says, slapping Mom five.

Then Charlie hugs my legs and says, "I know you can do it, Livi. You'll get on that show."

"Thanks, little man," I say, and slide into the car.

168

Neil and Charlie stand on the sidewalk and wave like crazy as Mom and I drive off.

It makes me feel good to know they're rooting for me, but when we get on the interstate, I feel tightness in my stomach. *What if I blow it? This is my one chance; I've got to make a good impression.* To stay calm, I run facts through my mind. *C. S. Lewis wrote the* Chronicles of Narnia. *There are 88 keys on a piano. Dad didn't call last Wednesday, like he was supposed to. The first televised sporting event was a 1939 baseball game between Columbia and Princeton universities.*

"Livi," Mom says, "want me to ask you trivia questions to relax you?"

"Sure." I put my hands in my lap and wiggle my shoulders. "Ready."

"This man invented the printing press." Mom knows to state the fact so that I can answer with a question.

"Who is Gutenberg?" I let out a breath. "Make them harder."

"I'll try." Mom taps the steering wheel. "This is the smallest U.S. state."

"Ugh, geography." But I know this one. "What is Delaware? No, that's not right. Delaware is the second-smallest state. What is Rhode Island?"

"Got it," Mom says.

As we drive, Mom hits me with her best stuff, but I

get them all right. And I realize I've stopped thinking about Dad, which is good, but my stomach is still roiled because I'm nervous about the audition. This is my only opportunity to get on Kids Week on *Jeopardy!* And there are lots of kids I'll have to beat to make it.

I don't understand how many kids until Mom and I arrive at the hotel in DC and walk into the ballroom. I remind myself there are only five hundred kids competing across the entire country. *Only* five hundred? And one-fifth of those kids and their families are here in this ballroom. The rest are at other audition sites across the country.

It seems like every one of the kids waiting is reading an atlas or trivia book. Neil was right. I should still be studying!

I squeeze Mom's hand as we walk through the ballroom and eyeball the other kids—the competition. "They look smart," I whisper.

She squeezes my hand and whispers, "You're smarter."

My legs feel weak and wobbly. *What if all the studying I've done isn't enough? What if there are a ton of geography questions, and not easy ones like Mom lobbed at me in the car on the way here?*

What if . . . I'm not good enough?

In the ballroom, lights dim and a large screen comes down from the ceiling.

Mom squeezes my shoulders, as if to say *This is it.*

I look at her and nod.

And just as if it's seven-thirty at home, Alex Trebek appears on the screen.

A few kids laugh. I cover my mouth, unable to believe this is happening.

"Welcome, kids and parents," Alex says. "You are in for what I hope will be a fun and memorable day."

Some kid says, "Hi, Alex," even though he's not really there, but I don't. I listen carefully as goose pimples ripple along my arms.

Alex explains how things will work; then members of the *Jeopardy!* staff, carrying clipboards, walk among us.

First, they take photos with Polaroid cameras, and we get to watch them develop. I look totally nervous in my picture, even though I'm smiling and have really good hair. Members of the staff collect the photos and attach them to our files.

I guess Mom was right. It does matter how we look.

On the big screen, Alex announces that it's time for parents to go into another room to learn behind-the-scenes information about *Jeopardy!* while we kids begin the testing process.

I get a funny feeling in my stomach when Mom goes, but she waves and mouths the words "Good luck," and I keep telling myself *You can do this. You will not freeze.*

"You're going to take a test now," Alex explains. The *Jeopardy!* staff gives everyone pen and paper, leads us to tables and chairs along the edges of the ballroom and tells us we can keep the pens when we're finished. I run my finger over the word "*Jeopardy!*" on my pen.

When we're seated and quiet, Alex Trebek quizzes us. He says the answers and we have to write the correct questions on our papers.

The questions are pretty easy. I think I get them all right, except for one geography question about a river in Africa. I wish Tucker were here to help. *Did I just wish Tucker were here?*

When the test is over, the *Jeopardy!* staff collects our

papers and we're taken into the room where our parents are waiting.

Mom grips my upper arms. "How'd you do?"

"Good, I think." Then I remember Dad's admonition on the phone awhile back. "Well," I say. "I think I did well."

"I knew you would, Livi." Mom hugs me hard. "What's next?"

"They said we're free to grab lunch while they score the tests."

Mom nods.

"I need to be back in the ballroom in two hours. That's when they'll post the results." I realize I'm crossing my fingers tightly, because in two hours, if I don't score well enough, I'll be heading home. And it will be over.

"Okay, then," Mom says.

"Okay," I say, uncrossing my fingers and letting out the breath I've been holding.

Mom hooks her elbow around mine, and we walk toward the hotel's main doors. "Shall we?" she asks, as though we're fancy ladies.

"Of course we shall," I say in my snootiest accent.

Outside in the cold air, I feel light and airy, like I'm finished, but the hardest part happens when we return. I read about it on the message boards. If I'm lucky and get a high-enough score to move forward—fingers, toes and eyeballs crossed—I'll need to ace the interview and practice game.

"Where should we eat, Livi?"

The question takes me by surprise, and I realize this will be the first time we've gone out to eat since Mom lost her job nearly four months ago.

This *is* a special day!

Who's on the List? (Part I)

When I look at the menu, I open my eyes wide to signal Mom that the prices are too expensive.

She closes her menu and leans toward me. "Livi, you've worked so hard to be here. Please don't look at the prices." She waves her hand dismissively. "Order whatever you'd like. Today, you get to be queen for a day. Olivia Bean, Trivia Queen."

I love the sound of that. *The Elizabethan era was named after the Queen of England, Elizabeth I.* Maybe someday, an era will be named after me. *Yeah, right!*

After we order—Mom gets a cup of tomato bisque and a mixed green salad; I choose a goat cheese, roasted red pepper and portobello mushroom sandwich with chocolate milk—Mom calls home and hands me the phone.

"Hi, Livi," Charlie squeaks.

His voice makes me melt inside. How can Dad not want to talk to him sometimes? "Hi, buddy," I say, hunching sideways so that I don't bother the people at nearby tables.

"Say hi to the president," Charlie says.

"Will do. Hey," I whisper. "Did you know the White House has a bowling alley inside it and a movie theater?"

"Cooooool. Wish I could be there with you, Livi," he whines. "Neil says it's Olivia Bean Day. Charlie Bean Day comes later. I say, *poop*!" There's muffled talking in the background; then Charlie's voice erupts: "Cookies, Livi! Gotta go."

"Bye, Char—"

"How's it going, Olivia?" Neil sounds genuinely excited for me.

"Great," I manage to say, but my throat squeezes and no more words make it through. Something about Neil asking about me—me! A bratty kid who was so mean to him, especially when he wanted to watch *Jeopardy!* with me—makes me want to cry. I sniff hard, feeling like the fancy people at nearby tables are staring at me. I wouldn't be sitting here if it weren't for Neil registering me. "Neil?" I say softly.

"Yes, sweetheart?"

The word "sweetheart" triggers my throat to constrict

again. "Thank you." I smooth out the cloth napkin covering the lap of my new skirt. "I mean it. Thank you . . . for everything."

"No need to thank me, Olivia. Just win, okay? We're pulling for you."

"Go, Livi!" Charlie screams from the background, but his words are garbled, like his mouth is stuffed with cotton. Or cookies. I smile at the image of Charlie squirreling cookie bits in his cheeks and spraying crumbs as he talks.

"See?" Neil says. "We're rooting for you. Go get 'em!"

"Will do," I say, and hand the phone back to Mom. My throat is still tight because it turns out my little bother isn't as much of a pain as I thought, and the person I believed was my archenemy for a long time has turned out to be a pretty good—albeit hairy—guy.

Our lunches arrive on china dishes. We share with each other; then Mom insists we get dessert to celebrate Olivia Bean, Trivia Queen Day.

Warm blueberry cobbler with vanilla ice cream never tasted so good.

While shoveling spoonfuls into my mouth, I mentally list the people who've helped me get here: Neil, who registered me. Mom, who decorated wreaths—her least favorite thing—to buy me new clothes, a haircut and our trip here. Charlie, who shared his gross trivia and his·

enthusiasm with me. And even Tucker, who grudgingly let me use his computer.

"You okay, Livi?" Mom's slender fingers land on top of mine.

I nod, but I'm not sure I am, because Dad is nowhere on my list.

Who's on the List? (Part II)

Back in the hotel ballroom, kids and their parents swarm around sheets of paper posted on the back wall. Some kids turn from the wall, sniffing, their parents leading them away. Even a couple boys swipe at their noses with shirt sleeves.

Panicked, I look at Mom.

She grabs my shoulders and looks me square in the eyes. "Livi, whatever happens, whether your name is on that list or not, you are an amazing human being and I'm proud of you." She kisses the top of my head. "And your big, beautiful brain."

I nod; then Mom steers me to where the results are posted.

It takes a while for enough people to move away that

I can scan the list. It's in alphabetical order, so my name is near the beginning.

My name is near the beginning!

I'm on the list of people who passed the test and get to stay for the interview and practice game.

I want to scream and jump around with Mom like we did when I got the phone call, but there are so many kids turning from the board, crying or looking like they're about to, that I hold it in.

There's a girl next to me who looks like she's about to burst, too.

"Did you make it?" she asks tentatively.

I nod. "You?"

She nods.

We hug each other like we've been friends forever. I think of Nikki and feel a pang.

"I'm Melissa," she says, tucking short, dark hair behind her ears. "I've *always* wanted to be on *Jeopardy!*"

"Me too," I say, thrusting out my hand. "Olivia Bean." *Trivia Queen.*

We shake like crazy, then crack up.

"Where are you from?" Melissa asks.

"Philadelphia. You?"

"Delaware."

The second-smallest state.

We find chairs near the wall with our moms and wait to get called for our interviews.

"I think I've read every book ever written about *Jeopardy!*," Melissa says.

"Me too," I say, even though I've read only the one Mom and Neil gave me for Christmas. *How many books have been written about* Jeopardy!?

"I'm homeschooled," Melissa says.

I almost say *Me too*, but I'm not homeschooled. "That's cool."

Melissa glances at her mom. "It's okay. The good thing about it is I can spend as much time as I want studying for *Jeopardy!*, and my mom doesn't care. Some days I'll study for *Jeopardy!* from the time I wake up until I go to bed. Right, Mom?"

"Right," her mother says. "You're a *Jeopardy!* machine, sweetheart. Totally unbeatable."

Unbeatable?

Mom catches my eye and raises her eyebrows, as if to say *Don't let these people frazzle you. Melissa might be a* Jeopardy! *machine, but you're Olivia Bean, Trivia Queen.*

These people *are* making me feel frazzled because Melissa has a distinct advantage over me. I spend most of my day in school, dealing with drama in the lunchroom, thinking about Tucker Thomas and occasionally doing actual schoolwork, but definitely *not* studying for *Jeopardy!*

Melissa continues. "When I watch the show every night, I usually get questions the grown-ups miss."

I *miss* most of the questions that stump the grown-ups. They're really hard. "That's fantastic," I say with zero enthusiasm in my voice. I wish I weren't sitting next to this new girl anymore.

There are only fifteen spots for Kids Week. Fifteen! And I get the distinct feeling Melissa is trying to psych me out so I'll mess up during my interview or the practice game.

Melissa isn't what I'd originally hoped—a potential new friend. She's my competition. Dad would probably tell me to watch out for her, tell me she'll try to trip me up. And I will be careful, because I'm not going to let Melissa get in the way of making it to California, to getting on the show. *To seeing Dad and Nikki.*

While our moms make polite conversation, Melissa glances at me. Her eyes narrow like she's sizing me up, and I wonder if she's thinking the same things about me.

Maybe I can psych Melissa out, too.

I smile broadly, then slouch in my chair, as though I don't have a worry in the world. As though I have no doubt I'll trounce the competition during the interview and practice game. As though I'm completely confident and relaxed, like Dad used to look when we watched *Jeopardy!* together.

But the truth is, I'm a nervous wreck.

What Do You Want to Be When You Grow Up?

By the time someone calls my name, I'm so tense I pop up like Punxsutawney Phil silently announcing six more weeks of winter. I blurt out "Here!" and wave my arm, as though I'm in a huge crowd instead of a quiet room with a few dozen kids and their parents.

"Little eager?" Melissa's mom says, laughing, as though she's making a joke.

But I know she's not, and my cheeks explode with heat.

Mom glares at her, then kisses my cheek and whispers, "Knock 'em dead, Livi."

Melissa grabs my hand and squeezes. "Good luck, Olivia. I hope you don't mess up."

When she lets go, I have to shake my hand out. She squeezed so hard it hurts.

"Me too," I mutter, even though now I *know* she's trying to psych me out. I hope I get picked because I have to visit Dad—he sounded so lonely that one time on the phone—and I'm tired of wiping my butt with sandpaper.

I hear someone call Melissa's name. She's going in for her interview, too.

As I walk toward my interview room, my stomach is a jangle of nerves. I tug on my blouse and skirt to make sure everything looks nice. I hope my hair hasn't resumed its usual flat state. *This is it*, I remind myself. *Smile. Smile. Smile.* But it's hard to force a cheerful smile when I feel so anxious.

A lady with a clipboard tells me to go over to a man sitting behind a table.

I shake his hand firmly, like Neil taught me, but not in a bone-crunching way like Melissa just did to me. "Hi," I say, "I'm Olivia Bean." And it almost feels like Mom and Neil and Charlie are standing behind me shouting, "Go, Livi! Go!"

I smile, but this time it's not forced.

The man smiles right away, and I hope that's a good sign.

"I'm Charlie," he says.

"My brother's name is Charlie. He loves gross trivia."

"Me too," Charlie says. "Must be something about guys named Charlie, huh?" He shuffles some papers.

"Anyway," he says, "I'm going to be your interviewer today."

"I'm Olivia and I'm going to be your interviewee." *Shut up, Bean Head! Charlie will think you're a raving lunatic.*

He chuckles. *Score!*

"Tell me, Olivia, what do you want to be when you grow up?" Charlie's pen is poised over a clipboard.

What do I want to be when I grow up? I know how many quarts are in a gallon—four—and how many bones are in the adult human body—206—but I'm totally unprepared for this question. My mind zips through options. I don't want to be a geography teacher, that's for sure. Or a vet or a model, like a lot of girls in my class say they do. I don't want to be an interpreter for the United Nations, like Nikki used to want to be. I wonder if she still does. *What do I want to be when I grow up?* My big, beautiful, three-pound brain blanks. I feel like I did onstage with the hula hoop around my waist.

Then it pops into my head: trivia. I love studying trivia. "A triviaologist," I say. *Is this the stupidest answer he's ever heard?* I suddenly remember Alex Trebek on the big screen earlier. "Or maybe a game show host, like Alex Trebek. That would be cool." I hope I said the right thing. I hope Charlie can sense how much I want this. Need this.

He writes something, then looks up.

"Speaking of Alex," Charlie says, "what will you say to him if you meet him?"

I bite my bottom lip. "Um, can I have your autograph?"

Charlie writes again. I wish he'd smile or look disapproving or something, instead of just asking questions and jotting notes after I answer.

"Why do you want to be on Kids Week?"

Do I tell him the truth? It's the only way I'll get to visit my dad. We need the money. But those answers don't feel right. I take a deep breath and say, "I've watched *Jeopardy!* every day with my dad until he—" I bite my lip to keep from saying more. *Should I mention Neil?* "People know they are in mortal danger if they bother me between seven-thirty and eight on weeknights. And I study trivia all the time. For fun."

I'm relieved when the interview is over and I can go back to Mom. I'm not happy to see she's still sitting with Melissa and her mom.

"How'd you do?" Melissa blurts out before I even sit.

I shrug, determined not to tell her anything. "You?"

"No idea," she says.

I'm sure she's lying. She probably answered the questions with sophistication and wit. She probably didn't say anything dumb, like *I want to be a triviaologist when I grow up*. Melissa even got done with her interview sooner and is probably well on her way to getting one of those fifteen spots.

There's an uncomfortable silence between us as we wait for the last kids to come back from their interviews.

When the staff announces that the mock *Jeopardy!* game will begin, I'm grateful at first.

I can't believe I'll finally get to be on *Jeopardy!*, even if it is only pretend.

But as soon as they make the announcement, Melissa leans forward and rubs her hands together, like she's ready to stomp the competition.

I gulp. *Am I?*

Who Is Not Alex Trebek?

I stand behind a table with a buzzer in my hand, facing pseudo–Alex Trebek, who is really a lady with a clipboard. *What is it with these people and their clipboards?*

The logical part of me knows it's not the real thing, that this is a mock game. But the emotional part of me is so excited because it *feels* like the real thing.

The boy to my left is sweating down the sides of his face, which is probably because he's wearing a tweed suit. And a bow tie. Dad would make fun of his bow tie. The girl to my right is chewing gum, her hand gripping the buzzer like she means business. She has bright pink hair and looks a lot older than twelve. This definitely isn't living room *Jeopardy!* with Neil or even Dad.

Focus, Jelly Bean. Dad's voice is in my head. *You've got to play to win. There's no other reason to get in the game.* I think of Neil and Charlie on the phone, encouraging me. And Mom, making all those wreaths so I could be here.

I can't let them down.

Who Controls the Buzzer?

I miss the first question—The profession of Nancy Drew's father. What is lawyer? —and the second—The smallest human muscle is found in these organs. What are ears? (I thought it was eyes.) I feel like I'm letting everybody down.

Win, Livi, win! Charlie's voice ricochets around my three-pound brain.

After the third answer—He wrote fourteen books about Oz.—I stab the buzzer with a vengeance and am shocked when I beat Bow Tie and Pink Hair and correctly answer, "Who is L. Frank Baum?" Then I do it again. And again. *I'm on fire,* as Dad says when he's having a winning streak in poker.

I can tell by my opponents' faces they know the answers, but I'm quicker pressing the buzzer. In the book

Mom and Neil gave me, I read that it's vital to have excellent reflexes with the buzzer. On the real game, the buzzer is actually referred to as a signaling device. And being quicker than one's opponents with the signaling device can make the difference between winning and losing.

And in this mock game, I'm winning.

I'm surprised when the game ends. It's much quicker than the real game. When it's over, I almost expect the lady with the clipboard to put her arm around my shoulders and tell me about the cash I've won. But she says, "Great job, kids. Thanks." Then she calls, "Bring in the next group."

That's it?

I shake the hand of the boy next to me—it's sweaty—and the girl on the other side. They don't look too happy with me. For a second, I feel like I did when I answered all the questions in the Brain Blaster battle between the girls and boys in school and everyone seemed annoyed with me.

But when I think about it, I don't feel upset now, because I did exactly what I was supposed to. I played aggressively and didn't freeze. I know Dad would be proud.

Someone from the show comes over and shakes my hand. "You did very well." She writes something on yet another clipboard, looks up and says, "Olivia Bean."

"Thank you," I say.

I imagine myself actually on the show with Alex Trebek. I see myself being first on the signaling device against two brilliant opponents. I imagine Mom and Dad rushing onto the stage after I win to congratulate me.

Yeah, right!

What are the odds I will get on Kids Week? There are five hundred kids just like me across the country, competing for fifteen measly spots. Kids like Melissa. Even if, by some miracle, I am chosen to appear on the show, what are the chances Dad would even come watch me on *Jeopardy!*? I hope 100 percent, but I'm not sure, with the way he's been acting.

I hear Dad's voice in my head. *You've got to play to win, Jelly Bean.*

I played, I think. But I doubt I can win. I mean really win, as in make it all the way to Culver City to appear on *Jeopardy!*

The woman who complimented my playing in the mock game leads me to where the parents are waiting.

And it's over.

What Are the Odds?

I talk a mile a minute to Mom as we drive away from the hotel, recounting every moment of the day in detail. There seems to be no barrier between my brain and my mouth. Soon, though, my energy leaks out, like somebody pulled a plug somewhere on me, and I can barely stay awake.

"You did good," Mom says.

I did well, I think, Dad's words in my head.

"Thanks." I watch Mom, her fingers tapping out a beat on the steering wheel. "For everything."

"You're welcome, Livi."

I close my eyelids, rest my head on my coat and grin. I can't wait to tell Tucker I kicked butt in the mock game. *Did I really just think that?* But the person I really want to tell is Dad. I hope he'll be proud of me. I even think of telling Carly, Brooke and Julia at lunch, but doubt I will. They're tired of hearing me talk about *Jeopardy!*, and I'm tired of hearing them talk about nail polish, boys and Bolivia.

I wake to Charlie shaking me with his skinny hands. "How'd you do, Livi? Are you going to be on TV? Wake up, Livi. Wake up!"

I blink.

Charlie, Neil and Mom stand outside the open car door, looking at me. A gust of icy wind smacks my face.

I shake my head. "Hi."

"How'd it go, Olivia?" Neil asks.

"Well," I say, still groggy. "I think."

"Hooray!" Charlie jumps and waves his arms windmill-style. "I'm telling all my friends Livi's going to be on TV. Woohoo!"

"Not yet," I tell him. "They pick only fifteen kids. I was really lucky just to get this far."

"That's all they choose?" Neil asks.

"Fifteen out of all those kids there today?" Mom says.

"No," I say. "Fifteen out of all the kids who went to auditions like that at five different hotels across the country."

Mom puts her palm to her forehead. "No."

"Yup." I nod. "Nearly impossible odds."

"Hey, at least you got this far," Neil says, patting my shoulder.

"Hooray, Livi!" Charlie yanks on my arm. "You're famous!"

It's nice to be surrounded by people who are excited for me, but the one I want to tell now is probably too busy. After we go inside and talk and Mom has a cup of tea, I take the phone to my room.

Dad isn't home, and I know I'm not supposed to call his cell, but I do.

"Dad? I know you don't like me to call your cell, but—"

"It's okay, Jelly Bean. What's up?"

When he calls me Jelly Bean, I know he's not mad. But I still feel choked up and I'm not sure why. "I auditioned for *Jeopardy!* today."

"You what?"

"Yup," I say, glad Dad sounds excited. "Mom drove me to DC, and I went to a hotel with about a hundred other kids. And she took me to lunch and—"

"Hang on a minute, Olivia."

There's muffled talking. I want to tell Dad about Melissa and how she tried to rattle me but I didn't let her. I know Dad will be proud of me for that.

"Sorry, honey," Dad says. "Go on. You went to DC."

"Yeah," I say. "I went with Mom and had to take a test. And Alex Trebek was on the screen. It was so funny, and—"

"Olivia, I don't mean to rush you. But is this going to take long? Stella and I are on the golf course."

Not today. Please don't rush me off the phone today.

"No," I say, feeling tightness in my throat. I've got to hurry and get to the good part. "A guy named Charlie interviewed me, and I told him I wanted to be a trivia-ologist. Stupid, right?"

"I don't think that's a real job," Dad says. "Look, baby, that sounds like fun, really cool, but I've got to run. Talk to you later, okay? I'll call soon. Promise."

But Dad doesn't wait for my answer. He hangs up. I picture him in golf pants, shirt and shoes, jogging across the green to Stella, who is probably wearing spiky heels that sink into the soft green with each step. Because that's the kind of person she is.

"Okay," I say to the dead phone. "Talk to you later."

But I doubt Dad will call back. In fact, I probably have better odds that the *Jeopardy!* people will call. Except I know that now it's not a phone call I'm waiting for. According to the message boards I read, what I need to hope for is the delivery of a FedEx envelope.

Come on, FedEx!

What's in the Envelope?

It's Valentine's Day—twenty-four days since the *Jeopardy!* audition in DC.

Mom puts a box of candy hearts next to my cereal bowl at the table and one next to Charlie's, too.

"Hurry up, little man," Mom calls. "Your cereal's getting soggy."

"One minute," he yells. "Be right there."

I drop a few candies into my cereal and wish I'd thought to give something to Mom or Charlie or even Neil.

Neil walks into the kitchen, wearing his ratty robe.

"You're not Charlie," Mom says, grinning.

Neil looks down at himself and says, "Right you are, you brilliant woman." Then he grabs Mom in a bear hug. "Who loves you, baby?"

Mom grins. "Beats me."

He ravages Mom with kisses on her neck. "You'd better know."

I get a little sick to my stomach. It's hard to see and hear things like that. It's still uncomfortable to know that the person hugging and kissing Mom isn't Dad. But then, maybe I'd feel uncomfortable even if Dad were kissing Mom's neck.

I'm grateful when Charlie zooms into the kitchen, but worry that Neil hugging Mom like that might upset him. Charlie doesn't even notice! He's waving a piece of red construction paper. "Here, Livi." On the paper is a giant eyeball cut from a magazine and a lopsided heart drawn in purple crayon.

"Happy Valiumtimes Day, Livi."

Neil's still holding Mom, and they both tilt their heads at Charlie.

"Happy Valiumtimes Day to you too, Charlie." I kiss his cheek, wishing again I'd at least made cards for everyone.

Charlie wipes off his cheek and says, "An ostrich's eye is bigger than its brain. But your brain, Livi, is bigger than an ostrich's eye."

"Thanks, Charlie." I pop a candy heart into my mouth. "I'm glad you're my little bother."

"Me too," he says. "And your big brain is going to get you on *Jeopardy!* That's what Neil says."

"I don't know, bud." I ruffle Charlie's hair. "It's been twenty-four days since the audition and an envelope hasn't arrived. Doesn't look good."

"You'll get on," Charlie says, slurping milk from his cereal bowl. "I know you will."

I wish I could feel as sure as Charlie, but each day the envelope doesn't arrive, I lose hope.

After we finish eating, Mom takes Charlie to the bus and Neil washes the breakfast dishes. I'm glad I don't have to do it. "Thanks, Neil."

"No problem, Olivia. Have a good day at school."

I'm already out of the kitchen, but I walk back in. "Neil?"

He turns from the sink, a scrub brush in one hand. "Yeah?"

"Happy Valiumtimes Day."

Neil nods. "You too, Olivia."

He's not my dad, but Neil's a good guy. He makes my mom happy, even though she still hasn't found a job. And Charlie adores him.

I throw on my coat, grab my backpack and head outside. A blast of icy wind smacks me in the face.

Tucker's already on the steps waiting, his nose red and eyes watering from the cold.

We've been walking to school together most days since he let me use his computer to take the online

Jeopardy! test. Sometimes while we walk, he quizzes me on geography facts in case the *Jeopardy!* people choose me to appear on the show. And Tucker hasn't called me Olivia Bean, Hula Hoop Queen even once since I told him how much I hate it.

"Here," Tucker says, thrusting a pink envelope at me.

It's the same shade of pink as the hair of the girl who played mock *Jeopardy!* beside me at last month's audition.

As soon as I take the envelope, Tucker rushes down the steps and heads toward school. Without me!

I shake my head and slide one frozen finger under the flap.

The card has an equation on the front: "1 + 1 = 2." Inside it says, "You're SUM friend." In handwriting below that is *Happy Valentine's Day, Bean. Your friend, Tucker.*

I put the card back into the envelope and push it deep inside my backpack. Then I jam stiff fingers into my coat pockets to warm them, hunch forward against the wind and walk to school with a definite bounce in my step.

Tucker doesn't look at me the entire day at school, but that's okay because I have his card in my backpack. And that says it all.

I expect him to walk me home after school, but he doesn't, and I can't believe I actually miss his company.

Walking home alone reminds me how much I still miss Nikki. When she and I walked home from school together, she'd imitate our teachers and make me laugh so hard I'd cry. I wonder who she's walking home from school with now.

I grab the house key from around my neck and think about calling her as I walk up our front steps. I've tried several times over the past two years. Mostly, Stella tells me Nikki is busy and can't come to the phone. But once, Nikki got on the phone and screamed, "I don't want to talk to you, Olivia. Don't you get that?"

I didn't get it and I still don't. *What did I do to her?* My father did something terrible—took her away from her home and from me. I get that. Oh boy, do I get that. *But I didn't do anything. Did I?*

When I reach the top step and open our storm door, a large cardboard envelope falls out.

A FedEx envelope.

When I bend to retrieve it with trembling fingers, I see it's addressed to "The Parents of Olivia Bean." And it has "Sony Pictures Studios, Culver City, CA" as the return address.

What Does Olivia Have to Tell Dad?

"They don't send FedEx envelopes for rejections," Mom says, in answer to my question. She looks at Neil. "Do they?"

Neil shakes his head. "I seriously doubt it."

"Open it already, Olivia," Mom says, squeezing her hands into fists.

"Yeah, open it, Livi," Charlie says, jumping like a human pogo stick.

I take a breath, then pull the tab on the back of the envelope. After removing a stack of papers, I read the top page—a letter—out loud.

"'Congratulations, Olivia Bean! You
are one of only fifteen children
selected . . .' "

Mom takes the papers and envelope from my hands and lays them on the coffee table in front of us. Then she grabs me and we jump and scream. Neil grabs both of us in a giant hug and joins us in the jumping and screaming.

"Hey!"

We turn and notice Charlie standing there.

Neil scoops him up. "Livi got onto *Jeopardy!*, buddy. Your sister's going to be on TV."

That's when I stop moving because I, Olivia Bean, am going to be on *Jeopardy!* The thing I've wanted almost my whole life is actually going to happen.

My legs feel weak, so I sit, afraid I'll collapse if I don't. Mom and Neil sit beside me. Charlie squeezes my neck so hard it hurts. "I told you, Livi. I told you! I told you! I have to pee."

Mom grabs Charlie and steers him toward the stairs. "Run, Charlie. Run."

Charlie runs.

Mom shakes her head. "I can't believe it. I can't."

Neil nods. "I can."

"Made it!" Charlie yells from upstairs.

"Hallelujah," Mom says, and we all crack up.

Charlie charges back downstairs.

"Flush!" Mom and Neil say at the same time.

He goes back up, flushes and runs down.

"Wash," Mom says.

Charlie runs up one more time, then comes down and collapses in my lap. "I told you, Livi."

Mom squeezes my shoulders. "I'm so proud of you. You worked so . . . You've wanted this for . . . I'm just so proud." Mom's eyes are wet and shiny.

I nod, feeling dazed and loved, not believing this can possibly be true.

"Proud. *Loud.* Cloud," Charlie sings. "Dowd. Rowd. Howd . . . y."

"Way to go, Olivia," Neil says, patting my knee. "I knew you could do it."

"Thanks." I stand. "I've got to tell Dad."

Who's Not Thrilled About Olivia's News?

In the kitchen, I crouch in a corner with the phone. Stella the Stealer answers, but gives Dad the phone without subjecting me to her phony, sugar-coated polite conversation.

"Hi, Olivia," Dad says. "What's up?"

He doesn't call me Jelly Bean or Butter Bean, but I can't worry about that now. "I got the letter, Dad," I whisper into the phone. "I'm going to be on Kids Week on *Jeopardy!*"

"That's fantastic!" Dad says. I picture him thrusting a fist in the air. "Olivia, that's the best news I've heard in a long time. Congratulations, sweetheart."

My chest swells with happiness from Dad's response.

Dad's voice sounds muffled when he says, "Olivia

made it onto *Jeopardy!*" Then I hear Stella say, "Tell her I said congratulations."

"Stella says congratulations."

"Thanks." My stomach twists; I don't want Stella's congratulations. I want to linger in the feeling of Dad being so excited for me.

"Oh, wait," Dad says. "Here comes Nikki."

My stomach goes into full clench. *Was I really thinking of calling her today?*

"Hey, Nik," Dad says. "Guess what?"

"We're moving to Alaska?" I hear Nikki say in the background. Her tone is snide and her voice sounds so much older than I remember.

"Ha-ha," Dad says, as though Nikki just made a hilarious joke, which she didn't. "Olivia is going to be on *Jeopardy!* Isn't that great?"

A pause.

I hold my breath.

"I'm thrilled for her," Nikki says in a flat voice. The only way she could have sounded *less* excited is if she were in a medically induced coma.

The air leaks out of my balloon. *What did I expect? Did I expect her to be happy for me? To decide we're suddenly best friends again?* I think of Tucker's sweet Valentine's Day card, still in my backpack, and realize that's exactly what I had expected. At least, that's what I'd hoped for.

Dad interrupts my thoughts. "Isn't *Jeopardy!* filmed here in L.A., Butter Bean?"

"Yes," I say, gripping the phone more tightly, feeling excitement creep back in. "Culver City." I decide I'm not going to let Nikki ruin my mood. At least Dad's excited for me. And that's miracle enough. Maybe if I could see Nikki, talk to her in person, we could find a way to work this whole thing out.

"Terrific," Dad says. "You'll come for a visit then."

It's happening. Everything I wanted is happening.

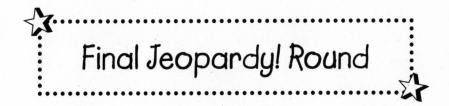

Final Jeopardy! Round

Which Planet Is Larger Than One Thousand Earths?

We're scheduled to fly to California the third week in March to record the Kids Week shows.

I have just over a month to prepare.

I practice the buzzer or signaling device by watching the real show in the evening with pen in hand. When Alex Trebek finishes reading an answer, I click the button on my pen as fast as I can. It's not the same as practicing with the real device, but it's as close as I can get. And I'll need lightning-fast reflexes to beat the competition.

I also stand while I watch the shows now because I'll be standing during the real thing. And I read in my *Jeopardy!* book that it helps recall if you create similar conditions under which you'll be quizzed.

Those kinds of practice no one can help me with.

But when it comes to filling my brain with as much information as possible, *everyone* helps.

Mom . . .

At breakfast, I find another stack of index cards beside my cereal bowl. These cards have a state's name on one side and its flower on the other. I read the name of the state and say the name of the flower before flipping the card to see if I'm right. I'm usually right.

Yesterday's stack of cards was presidents and their vice presidents. The day before that was well-known children's books and their authors. Before that, TV shows and the people who star in them.

Mom makes the cards every night before she goes to bed.

And car rides with Mom no longer involve normal conversation.

The other day, when she drove me to buy another new outfit to wear on *Jeopardy!*, I reached over to turn on the radio, but she grabbed my hand.

"Let's practice instead."

"Okay," I said.

"There are 5,280 of these in a statute mile."

"What are feet?" I ask.

"Correct."

"But a nautical mile is approximately 6,076 feet," I add.

Mom shakes her head. "You're amazing, Livi."

I blush, ready for Mom to hit me with the next question.

"A cow has four of these."

"What are stomachs?" I ask.

"How many—"

"But that's not exactly true," I say. "About the cow stomachs."

"Explain."

"There are four digestive compartments—the reticulum, rumen, omasum and abomasum. But the simple answer is four stomachs."

"Livi," Mom says, "you are so ready for this."

My heart pounds. My pits sweat. There are so many facts about so many different things. *How could I ever be ready for this?* "More questions, Mom!"

"This planet is larger than one thousand Earths."

"What is Jupiter?"

"Yes!"

Neil . . .

"Olivia," Neil calls when he comes home from work.

I hurry downstairs to find him carrying another stack

213

of library books. *Fish Facts*, *ESPN: The Mighty Book of Sports Knowledge*, *National Geographic Kids Almanac*, *Great Musicians*, *Weird but True: 300 Outrageous Facts* and *The 100 Best Poems of All Time*.

I take the pile of books upstairs and add them to the other piles of books Neil has brought home for me, and I resume studying. Until I realize I forgot something and run back downstairs.

Mom and Neil are cuddled together on the couch, talking. They look up at me.

"Thanks, Neil."

Neil nods. "There are more where those came from, Brainy Bean."

I smile at the nickname, nod and run back upstairs.

Even though it's after ten o'clock and I have school the next morning, I stay up another hour and a half poring over the new library books.

There's so much to learn.

Charlie . . .

While we eat dinner, Charlie says, "A cockroach can survive without its head for a week before it dies of starvation."

"I'll die of starvation," I say, "if you don't stop spouting gross trivia during dinner."

"In your lifetime, you'll shed more than forty pounds of skin."

"Charlie!" I say.

Mom puts her fork down. "Little man, *please* save your gross trivia until we're done eating."

Charlie pouts and crosses his arms. "I'm just helping stuff Livi's brain like everyone else."

Mom takes a deep breath. "Okay. Just try to keep the facts from being too . . . you know . . ."

"Disgusting?" Charlie blurts out.

"Exactly," Mom says.

"Actually, Charlie," I say, shoveling a forkful of black beans and rice into my mouth, "you never know when Alex Trebek might ask about headless cockroaches and shedding skin. Keep those gross facts coming."

Mom raises an eyebrow at me.

I shrug. *It's hard to feel important when you're five.* "Well, you never know what Alex Trebek might ask." I wink at my little bother.

Charlie sits up taller. "Okay, Livi. Remember how I told you flamingos pee on their legs to cool off?"

"Yes," Mom says in a low, menacing tone.

"Well, turkey vultures *poop* on their legs to cool off."

"*Charlie!*" we both scream at the same time.

Tucker . . .

Tucker promises to teach me geography every day after school, unless he has debate club. Because of my weakness in geography, I accept. Even though it does mean dealing with Tucker's dirty-laundry land mines strewn all over his bedroom floor.

Sitting on Tucker's bed, I study his wall map and try to remember the major rivers of the world, but when I close my eyes and repeat them, I forget most of the names.

"You stink at geography, Bean."

Even though Tucker's right, I say, "I'm getting better, though. Aren't I?"

"A little." Tucker swivels on his desk chair. "But you still stink."

I sit back on Tucker's bed, my head leaning on his giant wall map. I'm probably crushing Paraguay with my hair. Even though Dad thinks I'm hopeless at geography, I need to ask. "Tucker, do you think I can learn this stuff in time for *Jeopardy!*?" I bite my fingernail because I know how Dad would answer that question.

"Of course you can, Bean," Tucker says, spinning his chair in a complete circle. "First, you have me as a coach. Second, you're a total brain."

I'm shocked by Tucker's confidence in me because I certainly don't have any in myself.

"Here's an easy one," Tucker says. "What is commonly referred to as the birthplace of democracy?"

I shake my head. I know I've heard this before, but can't remember the answer.

Tucker raises his arms. "Bean, I've asked you this one before."

I bite my lip. "I know, but I can't remember."

"Athens. Athens, Greece."

"Oh, yeah," I say, sitting tall on the bed. "I forgot."

"Say it."

"Huh?"

"Say it out loud so you'll remember."

"Athens, Greece," I say.

"Athens, Greece, what?"

"Athens, Greece, is commonly referred to as the birthplace of democracy."

"Good," Tucker says, turning his computer to face me. "Now," he says, flipping it on, "there's this great website—mywonderfulworld.org. It will help. There are geography games and lots of cool facts."

"I like cool facts."

"Yes, you do," Tucker says. "Especially when they're cool geography facts. Right, Bean?"

I sneer. "Especially."

"You love geography. Right, Bean?"

I shake my head, throw my arms in the air and shout, *"I love geography!"*

"Everything all right up there?" Mrs. Thomas calls.

I fall back onto the bed, my cheeks burning.

Tucker laughs. "Everything's fine, Mom. Olivia's having a fit because she loves studying so much."

I kick Tucker; then we both laugh.

By the time I get home, I remember quite a few things. I remember that the birthplace of democracy is Athens, Greece. I remember the Great Lakes—Superior, Huron, Michigan, Erie and Ontario. And I remember that Tucker's eyes are a really nice shade of blue, although I'm pretty sure *that* fact won't help me on *Jeopardy!*

Dad . . .

Will Olivia Ever Be Ready?

I shove Phil into my suitcase, zip it and open the door to Charlie's room.

Mom's helping him pack. Actually, she's standing with hands on hips over Charlie's overflowing suitcase.

I clear my throat. "Get me from Tucker's house when we're ready to leave. Okay, Mom?"

She ignores me completely. "Charlie, you can't bring that many Matchbox cars. Put some back."

"What if I need them?"

"When will you need them?"

"Well—"

"Mom, I'm going to Tucker's. Get me when we're ready to leave."

"Okay, Livi," Mom says. "Charlie Bean, I'll give you

five minutes to choose your three favorite cars. Three. That's it."

I shake my head and run down the steps. My stomach's doing somersaults by the time I'm at Tucker's front door because I can't believe I'll be on a plane soon, heading to California. After I knock on the Thomases' door—I remember not to ring the doorbell, which I assume they'll *never* fix—Tucker opens the door and yanks me inside.

"Today's Olivia's big day," Tucker tells his mom. "We need to study more before she goes."

Mrs. Thomas puts down the newspaper she's reading. I can't help but think that Mom's column with her photograph is *not* in that newspaper anymore. "Good luck, Olivia," she says. "We'll be rooting for you."

"Thanks," I say.

As Tucker and I race up the stairs, past his photographs, I think about how different things were only a couple months ago. How much Tucker and I couldn't stand each other. How he didn't want me to come up to his room to use his computer to take the *Jeopardy!* online test. And now he's helping me study!

When we get inside his room and Rose is running like a maniac on her hamster wheel, I lean toward Tucker and kiss his cheek.

He reels back and trips over a pile of underwear. "Why'd you do that?" he asks, touching his cheek.

I shrug.

Tucker stares at me. "Well . . ."

"Well," I say. "We'd better study fast because I'm flying to California soon."

"Flying . . . ," Tucker says. "California."

I smack him on the shoulder. "Come on, it was only a dumb kiss on the cheek."

"Oh, yeah, I'm cool," he says. "Let's study."

But I can tell he's flustered because he messes up words while he quizzes me on countries and state capitals, and his cheeks flame crimson.

I miss the capital of North Dakota, which Tucker informs me is Bismarck. That's when I hear a knock on Tucker's front door. "Come on, Olivia. It's time to go to the airport."

Am I ready for this? It feels like all the blood drains from my face.

"Knock 'em dead," Tucker says, and lightly punches my arm.

"Thanks," I say, rubbing my arm as though he hurt me, but he didn't.

"You're ready," Tucker says, punching a fist in the air. "You are so ready, Bean."

"Am I?"

"Oh, yeah," Tucker says, leaning over and kissing *me* on the cheek. "You're going to kick butt on that show, Olivia!"

I raise my eyebrows in surprise.

Tucker grins. "Take that."

I touch my palm to my cheek.

"Olivia!" Mom yells from downstairs. "Come on!"

"Coming!" I yell back, but I don't budge. My heart's beating a million times a minute. (I know it's really beating about one hundred times per minute.) Does it feel fast because Tucker just kissed me or because I'm flying across the country to compete on *Jeopardy!*? I have a feeling it's the latter.

Am I ready to compete on Jeopardy!*?*

Am I ready for the tough geography questions?

Am I ready to see Dad? And Stella and Nikki?

Just like in *Jeopardy!*, everything feels like it's in the form of a question for me.

Do I know the answers?

You bet I do. Because no matter what Mom, Neil, Charlie and Tucker keep telling me . . .

I'M

NOT

READY!

Did You Know About Sharks' Teeth?

Charlie loves the airplane.

When the flight attendant asks, "What would you like to drink, sir?" Charlie giggles and says, "Did you know an octopus will eat its own arms if it gets really hungry?"

Without missing a beat, the flight attendant replies, "Did you know sharks keep growing new teeth their whole lives?"

Charlie's eyes widen. "Cool."

The man nods. "I was a bit of a trivia geek growing up, especially when it came to sharks. In fact, I have about a dozen sharks' teeth I've found on different beaches, and I always keep one in my pocket. I think it's lucky. Now, what would you like to drink, little man?"

"Ginger ale . . . with a side of shark's tooth." Charlie

giggles and kicks his feet, which prompts the man in front of him to look back over his seat and glare.

"You got it," the flight attendant says, giving Charlie a high five and ignoring the glaring passenger.

I order water with no ice because I read somewhere that there's more bacteria in airplane ice than in a toilet.

The flight is long—four and a half hours—but it goes fast because of the screen embedded in the seat in front of me. Charlie uses his to watch TV, but I discover an in-flight quiz full of trivia questions. Perfect!

I type in my screen name—"Brainy Bean"—and play against other passengers. Some people join the game and others drop out, but I play the entire time—it's excellent practice—except when the pilot talks and the game freezes. Guess what? I win every time. Me—Brainy Bean—against the grown-ups!

When the quiz finally goes off because we are beginning our descent into the Los Angeles airport, I lean back, nervous about what to expect on *Jeopardy!* Nervous about my geography knowledge, or lack thereof. (Tucker would be disappointed to know I got a couple geography questions wrong on the in-flight quiz.) But mostly, I'm nervous about seeing Dad and Stella and Nikki. What if I do something to annoy Dad right away, like I do sometimes on the phone with him?

On the other hand, what if Dad takes one look at me,

Charlie and Mom and realizes he's made a gargantuan mistake by leaving us? What if he decides to ditch Stella and come home?

I glance at Neil. His beard is neatly trimmed and he just got a haircut. He's holding Mom's hand and closing his eyes as the plane descends. *What would happen to Neil if Dad decided to come home?*

I'm completely lost in my thoughts when the plane bumps onto the ground and whooshes along the runway, pressing me back into my seat.

As we're getting off, or "deplaning," as they call it, the flight attendant gives Charlie a shark's tooth from his pocket. "Remember, this is lucky," he tells Charlie.

"Thanks," Charlie says, squeezing the tooth in his fist. Then he looks off to the side, as though he's thinking about something.

While we walk down the corridor toward baggage claim, Charlie presses the shark's tooth into my palm. "It's lucky, Livi."

Who Is Olivia Bean?

What's really cool is that when we go down the escalator toward baggage claim, a man in a suit and black cap holds a small white board. On the board, it says:

Who is Olivia Bean?

My name. And they put it in the form of a *Jeopardy!* question.

Mom grabs my hand, and I feel like I'm going to burst from nervousness and excitement and happiness all fighting it out inside my stomach.

The man with the cap helps us get our luggage from the baggage carousel and takes us out to a van that says "Music Express" on the side. The seats are plush purple and really comfortable.

As he drives us toward our hotel, Charlie points out the window and shouts, "Palm trees!"

"Palm trees," Mom says, leaning back in her seat and closing her eyes.

When the driver stops and gets our luggage out, he says, "There will be instructions for you at the desk when you check in, but today is yours to relax and get acclimated."

Neil slips some money into the man's hand, and we go in.

In our hotel room, there are two big beds.

"I'll bunk with Charlie," Neil says, putting a suitcase on the far bed.

"And I'll sleep with Livi," Mom says, squeezing my shoulders.

In the bathroom, there are tiny soaps and tiny shampoo and conditioner bottles. The towels are bright white and thick, unlike our thin, worn ones at home. I can't believe *Jeopardy!* is paying for all this for the four of us just because I did well on a few tests and an audition. They even gave us extra spending money, to have fun in California when we're not busy with the show.

While I'm in the bathroom, I remember overhearing Mom on the phone a couple weeks ago. It wasn't hard to figure out who she was talking to.

Mom said, "We need to get Livi new clothes and—"

There was a pause. And then she said, "I just thought you could help—" Another pause. Then Mom's voice got louder so it was easier to hear. "She's your daughter too, you know."

Thinking about Mom's argument with Dad squeezes my stomach into a knot, and I stay in the bathroom until Mom knocks on the door. "You okay in there, Livi?"

"Be right out," I call as I clutch my middle.

"Good," she says. "We're meeting your father downstairs in ten minutes."

The knot in my stomach gets much, much tighter.

How Many Head Hairs Do We Lose Each Day?

I slip into the new dress Mom bought me and brush my hair and teeth two times each.

When Mom keeps fussing over Charlie's hair, Neil takes her hands and looks in her eyes. "It'll be okay, Marion."

Mom nods.

We go downstairs to the hotel's restaurant.

Charlie's talking a million miles a minute, spouting trivia and asking questions. Mom shushes him and holds his hand and mine.

While we're waiting, people go into the restaurant and come out. They look happy.

We're quiet. Mom is holding my hand a little too tightly. From the look on Charlie's face, she's doing the same to his.

Dad appears through the doorway, and it takes my breath away. He's grown a beard, like Neil's, but Dad's is scraggly. He strides toward us, wearing cowboy boots and a tight black T-shirt tucked into jeans.

Mom gives my hand an extra-hard squeeze, but it makes me feel better. It reminds me she's here. Neil's here. Charlie's here.

Stella and Nikki, it seems, are not.

I let out a big breath and finally pay attention to Charlie. He's standing like Pinocchio. He's rigid and his eyes are wide. He's looking at Dad as though he's seeing a stranger. I want to grab Charlie and hug him so he won't be scared, but I don't move.

"You grew a beard," Mom says.

Dad strokes the hairs on his chin. "I figured if I was losing it on top, I'd better grow it down here." He laughs, but no one else does. "Yeah, Stella keeps nagging me to shave it off, but . . ."

Charlie pops out with, "A human being loses between forty and one hundred hairs a day."

Now everyone laughs. Nervous laughter, but it feels good, like pressure had been building and Charlie figured out how to open a release valve.

"He's a Bean, all right," Dad says, and scoops Charlie up for a tight hug.

Charlie's eyes grow wide.

What about me? I'm here too.

Dad puts Charlie down and shakes Neil's hand. "Neil."

Neil says, "Bill."

Hello? You haven't even spoken to me yet.

"Marion." Dad nods at Mom.

Mom nods back, then turns away.

Maybe I'm invisible.

Suddenly, Dad whirls around and kneels in front of me. "And how's my Butter Bean?" He grabs me in a squeeze, then pulls back to look at me. "You ready for *Jeopardy!*?"

There in Dad's arms, just like old times, I feel ready for anything.

What Question Is Too Hard to Ask?

The question flies from my mouth as though it's a casual thought. It's not. "Where's Nikki?"

Dad waves off the question like it's completely inconsequential. It's not. "Nikki had a . . ." Dad runs a hand through his hair. "She had something to do with Stella. That's all. Nothing to worry about, Butter Bean."

I'm not worried. I just figured that if I flew all the way across the country, she could at least come out and meet me for dinner.

Dad tousles my hair, like I'm five years old, and it annoys me.

"So, shall we get a seat?" Dad asks, rubbing his hands together.

"I was really hoping to see her," I say, not willing to let this drop.

Dad signals the hostess with a raised arm. As she walks over, he pulls his cell out of his pocket and hands it to me. "Call her. I'm sure she'd like to talk to you."

I'm sure she wouldn't.

With the weight of Dad's phone in my hand, I reconsider. Nikki obviously hates me. "That's okay," I say, trying to give the phone back. "We're going to be eating now, anyway."

Dad waves me off. "Go right out there, Butter Bean, and call her. It's about time you two started talking again."

I look at Mom.

She nods, so I go outside the restaurant. People are milling around, and I'm not comfortable having this conversation in such a public place. I find a bench and hunch over as I press the numbers.

When Nikki answers, I suck in my breath so hard I almost choke.

"Hello?" Nikki says. "Bill, is this you? You okay?" I think I hear her mutter, "Moron."

It doesn't sound like something Nikki would say, but it's definitely her voice.

After one good cough, I can speak. "It's me," I say.

I'm greeted by dead silence.

"Hello? Nikki?"

Nothing.

"Please say something. I came all the way to California and—"

"What do you want me to say, Olivia?" Nikki snaps. "That I'm so glad you're here? That I hope we can be best friends again?"

I kind of do hope she'll say those things and we can go back to the way we were.

"Well, that's not going to happen."

Sucker punch to the gut. I lean over even more, feeling like passersby can hear the mean thing Nikki just said. "Why?" is the only word I can push past my tight throat.

"Why?" she says and laughs, but it's a mean laugh, one that says I'm too stupid to understand. Even though Nikki and I are the same age, she seems so much older now.

"Olivia, get a clue. Don't you realize your dad took me away from everything?"

I think about this. "He took you away from me and—"

"Everything."

I'm confused. Nikki didn't seem to love school *that* much. I take a deep breath and hope I don't start crying right here outside the restaurant. "What everything?" I ask, sounding like an idiot.

"Olivia," she says, in this barely controlled voice. "Let me tell you how life is here. Okay?"

"Okay," I whisper, not wanting to hear. Wanting to hang up and join my family for dinner and forget I ever called. But I don't. I sit, trembling, and listen to my former best friend tear my heart out.

"Eighteen times this school year, Stella forgot to pick me up after school. Eighteen times! And we live like two miles from the school, which is a really long walk. But no way I'm going on the bus with all those druggies."

I swallow hard. *Where do they live?* "Oh," I say, remembering a couple times that Nikki's mom forgot to pick us up when we were at the mall, and my mom had to get us.

Nikki continues. "When I fell down the steps running to Spanish class last month, the nurse couldn't reach Stella. Of course she couldn't reach her. She was getting a massage at some fancy place with your dad and had her phone turned off."

"Oh," I say again, in a small voice. I remember when Nikki and I were racing down our block and Nikki fell and cut a hole right through the knee of her jeans and was bleeding like crazy. I helped her walk home, but her mom wasn't there. Back at our house, my mom cleaned her knee, put on a bandage and found her a pair of jeans to wear.

Even though I want to press my palms against my ears so that I don't have to hear another word, Nikki, apparently, isn't finished. "Did you know that right after we moved here, your dad and Stella decided to go on a little honeymoon in Vegas for four days and left me here alone? I was ten!"

I gasp.

"Yeah," she says. "Want me to go on?"

I'm crying now, soft sobs that make my shoulders jerk. "No," I say. I sniff hard, hoping no one stops to ask if I'm okay. "I'm sorry," I say. "But I don't get what any of this has to do with me. We were best friends."

"Don't you get it?" Nikki asks. She's crying now, too. But I can tell she's more mad than sad.

I wrack my brain. It's filled with a million facts, but not one of them can help me figure out why Nikki hates me so much. "No, I don't get it," I say a little louder than I mean to. "I don't get why you hate me. I never did anything to you."

"You did," she says, sniffing hard. "It's totally not your fault and I know that. But still, I can't let it go."

"What?" I feel like shrieking. "What did I do to make you hate me so much?"

There's silence; then Nikki says five flat words that cut me like broken glass.

"You got the good parent."

"What?"

She sighs. "Your mom was like a mom to me, Olivia.

240

She cared about me more than . . ." Nikki chokes on her own words. "More than my mom ever did."

I start to say something to protest, but don't. Pictures flash in my mind of my mom cooking Nikki dinners, tucking us both in during sleepovers and giving Nikki a pad and a long talk when she got her first period at our house when she was only nine and a half. Mom even yelled at Nikki once for like fifteen minutes when she came to pick us up at the mall and saw Nikki talking to some creepy guy who had said he wanted to get her into modeling.

"I get it," I say in a quiet voice.

"Do you?" she says in a mean tone.

"Yes," I say, "I get why you're so upset, but I don't get why that means we can't still be friends. Why you can't even talk to me."

"Because . . ." Nikki sobs, and I want to reach through the phone and hug her, even though what she said was so hard to hear. "Because it hurts too much to talk to you, Olivia. To be reminded of everything I lost. Of what you still have."

"But I—"

She hangs up.

Who Wants Ice Cream?

I don't call Nikki back, even though it's my first instinct. I want to tell her she can call me and Mom anytime, that she can visit us too, but I know there's not money for that. I want to tell her that if I win on *Jeopardy!*, I'll buy her a plane ticket, a dozen plane tickets.

But it doesn't feel right. Nikki doesn't want to talk to me. Doesn't want to be reminded. Is it fair to make her feel bad just because I want to talk to her?

I take a deep breath and rush into the restaurant's bathroom. I stay in the stall awhile, wiping away tears, waiting for my face to feel less hot and prickly. I go over the conversation in my mind again and again. Maybe someday things will be different. I'm sure they will. But for now, I feel like I have to respect Nikki's wishes since

I can't change the way things are. I wish Stella weren't such a lousy mom. I wish Dad were a better parent to her.

To me. And Charlie.

I remember that Dad is only a few yards away from me. Dad. I pat cold water on my face, dry off with a paper towel, fling open the bathroom door and walk into the restaurant to find my family.

"Hey, Butter Bean," Dad says, scooching over to make room for me beside him.

My heart thumps. I slide in next to my dad and give him back the phone.

"Did you talk to Nikki?" he asks.

I feel Mom looking at me.

I nod, hoping I don't start crying again.

Mom must sense how I'm feeling because she pushes the bread basket toward me. "Eat something, Livi."

I shake my head because I'm not hungry, but decide to shove a piece of bread into my mouth to keep myself from crying.

Neil reaches over and pats my hand. This makes me want to cry even more.

"The mahimahi here is excellent," Dad says, his head behind the menu.

"Sharks eat mahimahi," I say, sniffing.

"Somebody's ready for *Jeopardy!*," Dad says.

I know he means it as a compliment, but I get annoyed. I think of how everyone at the table helped me prepare except him. How he couldn't even call when he was supposed to. How he took Nikki away from everything she cared about but didn't give her anything she needed.

I scooch a tiny bit away from Dad and touch the shark's tooth in my pocket. I look at Charlie. He's got his head on his hand while he looks at his menu.

"Hey, Charlie," I say. "You getting the mac and cheese?"

He closes his menu and nods.

"With salad?"

"Applesauce," he says.

"Good choice, little—"

"He's reading?" Dad asks.

"He's been reading for a while," Mom says. She doesn't say what she's probably thinking: *If you paid more attention to him, you'd know that.*

"Charlie reads trivia books," I tell Dad.

Dad nods and goes back to his own menu.

"You rock, little man," Neil says, and Charlie's face lights up.

Neil winks at Charlie.

I look at Dad. His face is hidden behind his menu.

During dinner, Dad tells gambling stories. How he almost won this and should have won that. How he won $4,700 at poker in Las Vegas last month but gave it all back and then some. And how mad Stella was.

By the time we're finished eating, Charlie yawns openly.

Dad taps him on the head. "Your old man boring you?"

"He's tired from the flight," Neil says, pulling Charlie closer to him.

Charlie has his head on the table. He lets out a big, noisy yawn.

"Tired, pal?" Neil asks.

Charlie nods, his head still on the table.

"C'mon, buddy," Dad says. "It's only six o'clock. I was going to take you and Livi out for ice cream."

I realize if we don't go out for ice cream, Dad will go home. And even though he's not always there for us, I really want to spend as much time as I can with him. After all, I worked really hard to get out to California.

"It's nine o'clock for him," Mom says, putting a hand on Charlie's neck. "Which is half an hour past his bedtime."

"Yeah," Neil says. "Dinner took a long time."

I feel annoyed at Neil for saying this, like he's insulting

Dad in some way. I want to say *I'll go out for ice cream,* but I don't.

The check comes and it sits in the middle of the table. And sits. Until Neil picks it up and says, "I'll get this one."

"Thanks, Neil," Dad says, folding his napkin.

Mom's lips pinch together.

I swallow hard, thinking about how tight money has been. I hope the extra spending money *Jeopardy!* gave us covers the cost of dinner.

"Well, I'd better hit the dusty trail," Dad says. He looks at Mom. "Since Charlie's so tired."

I want to scream, *What about me? Let's go out for ice cream, just you and me, Dad.*

"Oh, wait!" Mom says as Dad stands.

I'm glad she's keeping him here a little longer. Maybe he'll decide to take just me out for a while.

Mom reaches into her pocketbook and pulls out a cardboard ticket. "Here," she says, handing it to Dad. "This was in our packet when we arrived."

As Dad takes it, their fingers touch.

Mom pulls her hand away. "It's a ticket to see Livi on *Jeopardy!*"

Dad winks at me. "I'll be there. You can take that to the bank."

And he's gone.

There is a feeling of disappointment in the pit of my stomach. Why didn't he realize I'm older than Charlie and not at all tired? Why didn't he realize I came all the way out here to see him and would have loved to go out for ice cream . . . or whatever, as long as I was with him? The feeling of disappointment grows into an ache.

I wonder if this is how Nikki feels all the time.

Who Is NOT the Red Umbrella?

The next morning, all the families meet the "Music Express" van outside our hotel lobby.

Just the kids get on the van. The families have the day off to do whatever they want. That's what it says on the schedule. Mom, Neil and Charlie are going to Disneyland! I thought I'd be jealous, but I'm so excited to visit the *Jeopardy!* set that I'm happy for them.

On the bus to the studio, I look at the other fifteen kids in the van (there is one alternate in case someone gets sick or can't do the show for some reason) and realize Melissa didn't make the cut. I'm surprised but, I have to admit, also a little glad. I wouldn't want her trying to psych me out before my taping. I hope these kids are nicer than she was.

I slide onto a plush purple seat next to the window

and watch Mom and Neil lift Charlie up by his hands and swing him between them as they walk back into the hotel.

"Hey," a boy from the back shouts, "who is the only American president who was never married?"

"James Buchanan," someone shouts.

"Easy," says another kid.

A bunch of kids laugh. So does the driver.

I take a deep breath and my shoulders relax.

The girl across the aisle from me says, "Okay. Who wrote *Charlotte's Web?*"

"E. B. White," two kids shout at the same time.

"Hey, that was on the test," another kid says.

I smile, remembering the test. The online test that I took in Tucker's room with my feet nearly frozen. That seems such a long time ago. I remember changing my answer for that question to "Elwyn Brooks White."

"Elwyn Brooks White," I shout.

"Oooh. Good one," the boy from the back says.

"Totally," another girl says.

A few other kids nod at me.

My chest swells. I look around as we pull out of the parking lot and realize that on this van with these kids, I'm definitely *not* the red umbrella.

What Is $15,000?

At the studio, the contestant coordinator, Maggie, takes us into a room where we fill out paperwork and get another free pen. Maybe I'll give this one to Tucker. Or Charlie. I reach into my pocket and touch the shark's tooth he gave me.

After that, we're led into a room where we crowd around a table with bagels and cream cheese, bananas, milk, orange juice and even hot chocolate. A man takes photos of us.

"Breakfast," Maggie announces. "Then we'll show you around the studio, let you get a feel for how the game will work tomorrow and give you some instructions."

My stomach is a jumble of nerves and excitement, but I take a bagel with cream cheese and a glass of orange juice and sit with the other kids.

While we eat, we talk about our hobbies and where

we're from. A boy from Ohio collects Pez dispensers and has over two hundred of them. The girl who sat across from me on the van has a black belt in tae kwon do. (Mental note: Do not get on her bad side.) All of us have watched *Jeopardy!* since we were little, except one boy who just started watching this past year.

I know two of these kids will be my competition tomorrow, but right now, I feel so comfortable with them, like we could all be friends if we lived near each other.

I wish school could be like this. It would be so nice to feel like I fit in. Before we're even done eating, we agree to exchange information and keep in touch with each other when this is over. I hope we do. It will be nice to have some new friends. Friends who don't obsess about Bolivia and nail polish and boys. Friends who care about the same things I do. Friends who don't make fun of me for being smart. Friends who don't live three thousand miles away . . . and hate me.

The set is not as big as it looks on TV. I can't believe I'm standing behind Alex Trebek's podium. But I am. A man holds a giant microphone over my head. Another man holds a camera. And a lady stands near them, telling me where to look. A bright light shines in my eyes, and I have to answer questions, like what I want to be when I grow up. This time I say, "A game show host, like Alex Trebek."

The lady smiles.

We do a fun skit together that will be used to encourage other kids to take the online test.

When we get a chance to practice with the buzzer, I grip it like the pen I used at home and press the black button with my thumb.

We even have to practice using the light stylus pen to write our names. I make my name neat and clear: *Olivia Bean*. I'm tempted to write *Brainy Bean*, but I know it would look like I'm showing off, so I resist the urge.

Maggie tells us that all five shows will be taped tomorrow. After each show, Alex will change into a new suit so that it looks like the shows are taped on different days.

I love getting this insider information.

And I can't wait to meet Alex Trebek!

It's so much fun that I'm bursting with excitement when we're dropped off at the hotel.

Mom, Neil and Charlie meet me in the lobby.

"I made a load of new friends," I say. "And the set is really cool. And they fed us really good food. And—"

"Mom and Neil took me to Disneyland," Charlie says. "I didn't throw up even once."

I hug Charlie. "That's great."

"No," Mom says. "It's really amazing because your brother ate cotton candy, a giant soft pretzel and ice cream, and gulped down two big sodas . . . plus lunch!"

I tousle my bother's hair and wonder if the spending

money the show gave Mom was enough to cover Disneyland and dinner last night and everything else they have to buy. Because I know we don't have any extra to pay for those things.

I shake my head and remind myself that tomorrow I'll have a chance to earn some money. A lot of money. Money that can really make a difference. The first-place winner is guaranteed fifteen thousand dollars plus a family vacation. Fifteen thousand dollars! That's probably more than Dad ever won gambling.

I make up my mind I'm going to win that money tomorrow. I'm going to press the buzzer faster than my opponents. I'm going to access the information in my brain more quickly. And when I win, I'm not going to buy video games or computers, like some of the other kids said they would.

I'm going to take Charlie, Mom and Neil to the mall and let them buy anything they want. I plan to spend a lot of time at the bookstore, buying all my favorite titles. And I'm going to buy about a thousand rolls of really soft toilet paper!

Then I'll put some money away for college. And Mom will get everything that's left over.

But first . . . I have to win.

Who Is the Hula Hoop Queen?

Today, when we get into the van, we're all quiet. We nod to each other, but no one calls out trivia questions.

Today, we are friends, but we are also competitors.

When we arrive at the set, we're told that they'll take groups of three kids at a time until all five shows are taped. No one knows which group he'll be in or when he'll be called. All we know is that we get only one chance. Unlike the adult games, on Kids Week, there are no champions. Even if you win, you don't return for the next game.

We wait.

I chew on my fingernails, unable to believe this is actually happening. I'm really going to be on *Jeopardy!*, the show I've loved watching since I was little. The show

Dad and I watched together night after night. Our special thing to do together. And now Dad will be in the audience watching me.

I'm so glad Mom, Neil, Charlie and Dad will be here. Especially Dad. With all of Tucker's tutoring, I can finally prove to him that I can be good at geography. I wish Tucker could be here, but he'd probably be a dumb butt and shout out answers or something he's not supposed to do. Maybe I can invite him over to watch the show in a couple months when it airs.

Oh, I hope I win.

I look around at the other kids, some bent over, some pacing, some muttering facts to themselves, and know they want to win as much as I do.

Maggie strides in with her clipboard and reads the names of the three kids in the first group.

"Jacob Andrews, Samantha Goff and Olivia Bean."

Olivia Bean? My eyes go wide and my pits erupt in sweat. I try to remember how many bacteria are in each square inch of armpit, but can't. *Oh, no!* My big, beautiful brain can't go blank now! I grip the shark's tooth in my pocket and follow Maggie and the two other kids toward the set.

Toward the Jeopardy! *set!*

I'm positioned behind my podium on the left side,

farthest from the audience. I hold on to the sides of the podium to still my shaking hands. I think that standing on the left side is a good omen because on the adult shows, the left side is the returning champion's spot.

I remind myself what Maggie told us: *Smile. Smile. And please, whatever you do, smile. Look like you're having the time of your life, even if you feel like you might throw up.*

So, even though no one is talking to me and we're not actually doing anything except waiting, I smile so hard my face hurts.

Maggie also said, "Don't look at the audience. I guarantee your parents are out there, so please don't look in that direction."

I break this rule.

The lights are bright and it's hard to see, but I scan the audience quickly. I spot Mom, Neil and Charlie. There are no empty seats next to them. Maybe Dad is sitting somewhere away from them. Maybe he arrived late and there were no spaces next to them.

The show hasn't begun yet, so I keep smiling and look more carefully at the audience.

There are no empty seats; Dad's not here.

I'll be there. You can take that to the bank.

I face the category board, like I'm supposed to. The show is about to begin.

Dad's not here. He didn't come.

I stop smiling.

Even though I'm supposed to pay attention, I can't help thinking about my fifth-grade talent show instead.

I'm standing backstage, just beyond the curtain, waiting for my turn to go on.

Lauren Garcia sings "Amazing Grace." Even though her voice cracks twice during the song, she gets thunderous applause.

That means I'm next. After weeks of practicing my hula hoop routine every single day after school, it's finally my turn.

I walk onto the dusty stage wearing a black bodysuit, stockings and dance shoes. I twirl my purple hula hoop on the fingers of my right hand as my music comes over the sound system. *"Everybody was kung fu fighting."*

I move the hula hoop down to my neck and keep it twirling. The audience gasps. I'd practiced this routine so many times, making little adjustments, adding fancy new moves, making sure I could keep the hula hoop spinning throughout the entire song.

I turn in a little circle onstage while the hula hoop spins around my neck. Waiting offstage is Tucker Thomas, dressed in a suit and tie. He has a big stain on the lapel of his suit jacket.

As I twirl the hoop around my neck, Tucker waves his saxophone at me from backstage and gives me a thumbs up.

I smile, but don't wave back. I can't or I might drop the hula hoop, and that would be humiliating, especially after how long I practiced. And with everyone in the audience watching.

The song keeps going: *"It was a little bit frightening."*

I face the audience and shimmy the purple hoop down to my waist. Another little gasp from the audience and some applause. I feel like I'll burst with happiness.

I notice the first place trophy off to the side and think that maybe this is the year I'll win it.

The spotlight shines brightly, but I can still see the audience. There are a lot of empty seats.

I spot Mom. Charlie is on her lap. I want to wave to Charlie but I keep going, following the routine I'd practiced.

I notice the seats on either side of Mom and Charlie are empty.

Dad had left us only a week before, after he and Mom had the most explosive fight ever.

"You're never here!" Mom screamed.

"Well, now I really won't be here, Marion," Dad retorted.

After Mom stormed up the steps and into Charlie's

room, I joined Dad downstairs on the couch. I felt bad that Mom had Charlie and Dad was alone.

Dad forced a smile and put his hand on my shoulder. "Don't worry, Butter Bean," he said. "I'm moving in with a friend, but I promise things won't change much. Okay?"

I nodded, believing Dad. I thought after Dad stayed with his friend awhile, he'd come back and work things out with Mom. They'd had plenty of fights before and always patched things up.

This was before I knew Dad was flying all the way across the country with Stella. And taking my best friend with him. So even though Charlie cried all the time and even Mom cried that night, I didn't cry. Not once.

The day after Dad moved out, he called and promised he'd be at the talent show, cheering me on. *He promised.*

But Dad isn't in the school auditorium, cheering me on.

Up there onstage, with the spotlight shining on me and all the people in the audience looking at me, with that stupid hula hoop spinning around and around me, fat tears drip down my cheeks. And I can't stop them.

I keep looking at the empty seats, thinking that Dad should be in one of them.

The music keeps going. At this part, I'm supposed to fling my arms out in karate-chop motions while the hula hoop spins around my waist. I'm supposed to get the hula hoop back up to my neck, then down again. I'm supposed to do my grand finale with the hula hoop spinning on one finger while I take a deep bow.

That's the way I choreographed it. That's the way it's supposed to happen.

Instead, I stare out at the empty seats while tears dribble down my cheeks, plunking onto the dusty stage floor. There I am, spinning and crying, spinning and crying. Until I stop moving and the hula hoop clatters to the stage.

There's a collective gasp from the audience.

I take one last look at the seats on either side of Mom and Charlie—empty—grab my hula hoop and run offstage.

Tucker says something to me, but I keep running.

What did he say? I know I heard it, but I can't remember.

Then, after all this time, standing on the set of *Jeopardy!*, I remember. I can hear Tucker's words drift out to me as I run past. *Olivia Bean, you're still the Hula Hoop Queen.*

That's what Tucker said. He called me the Hula Hoop Queen, but he hadn't said it in a mean way. He said it softly. Nicely. He'd meant it as a compliment, not an insult. All this time, I had thought he used those words as an insult.

"This is *Jeopardy!*"

Johnny Gilbert's voice. The show is starting.

But all I can think about is crying onstage during the talent show because Dad didn't show. And he's not here, either. *Jeopardy!* was his thing. Our thing. My throat tightens.

"And from Canton, Ohio, is Jacob Andrews. He likes playing basketball and acting, and he hopes to own a business someday."

They're moving down the line.

"From West Palm Beach, Florida, is Samantha Goff. Samantha has run in a half marathon. And someday she hopes to be president."

I'm next. But I can't move. Can't smile. Can't do anything.

Dad didn't show. Just like at my talent show in fifth grade.

Am I going to freeze now, too? Run off the stage and cry?

"And from Philadelphia, Pennsylvania, is Olivia Bean. Olivia loves trivia and wants to be a game show host when she grows up."

"*Go, Livi!*" Charlie screams.

Charlie's voice snaps me out of my trance. I look right into the camera and give the biggest smile of my life.

Charlie wants me to win. So does Mom. And Neil. And me! I want to win. I, Olivia Bean, want to win this game more than anything in the world. And Tucker back home wants me to win too.

"And now, here's the host of *Jeopardy!*," Johnny Gilbert's voice booms. "Alex Trebek."

I hold my breath as Alex Trebek strides onstage, and I think I'm going to faint.

What Animal Is Found in
the Swamps of Florida?

Alex announces the six categories: "Have You Got Game?, A Is for Animal—these are animals that begin with the letter A, Presidents, Am I Red?, That's Entertainment and Science Says."

The game begins so quickly. I'm not ready.

Samantha Goff chooses A Is for Animal for $100. Only she says "Animal for one hundred" because Maggie told us to pick one main word from the category instead of saying the whole thing. It makes the game go faster.

And it does go fast.

Alex says, "This type of animal named Arthur is a favorite children's book character."

Samantha buzzes in first and says, "What is an aardvark?"

I didn't even press the buzzer.

Head in the game, Olivia. Play to win. I realize the voice in my head is Dad's. But that's okay. Because I want to win.

"Animal for two hundred," says Samantha.

"This animal is often found in the swamps of Florida," Alex says.

The moment he finishes asking the question, I press the buzzer.

"Olivia?"

"What is an alligator?"

"That's correct," Alex says.

"Animal for three hundred," I say, feeling especially proud that I answered that question even though Samantha is from West Palm Beach, Florida. *Take that!*

I finish off the category, getting the rest of them right—"What is an ape?" "What is an anteater?" and "What is an armadillo?" Charlie told me armadillos can smell beetles, larvae and ants six inches underground and spend their days digging for and eating them. He also said armadillo poop looks like clay marbles, but that's not important now.

My thumb is all over that buzzer. I dominate the board, but Jacob is close and Samantha still has a good chance.

There's a commercial break. It's about the trip that today's winner and family will get—a cruise to Alaska.

They show a family standing on the side of a ship, whale watching. How much fun would that be? Now I want to win more than ever.

When the commercial break ends, Alex is standing next to our podiums.

I'm so nervous while he talks to Samantha and Jacob, but I keep smiling, like we were taught yesterday.

"Olivia?"

I nod.

"I understand you have a younger brother who loves trivia too," Alex says.

"Yes," I say. "Charlie's only five, but he loves gross trivia."

The audience laughs.

"Can you give me an example?"

I don't want to talk about flamingos peeing on their legs or armpit bacteria, so I say, "A cockroach can live without its head for a week."

"That's pretty gross," Alex says. "But interesting."

I smile because I know out in the audience, Charlie is loving this. I have no idea how Mom and Neil are keeping him from shouting or running onto the set. It probably involves physical restraint and promises of chocolate.

As Alex strides back to his podium to begin the Double Jeopardy! round, where dollar values are doubled, I touch the shark's tooth for luck.

Unfortunately, it doesn't work.

Jacob is much faster on the buzzer and gets a lot of the questions, but Samantha answers the big-money questions near the bottom of the board.

I get the leftovers, like "This person wrote *Little Women*" ("Who is Louisa May Alcott?") and "Dr. James Naismith first invented this game using a ball and two peach baskets" ("What is basketball?").

I know a lot of the other answers, but don't buzz in fast enough. I wish I had practiced even more clicking my pen at home. Being fast on the buzzer is so important, but so is being brave when betting. And I do that when I'm lucky enough to land on a Daily Double.

Jimmy, from the Clue Crew, shows a gorgeous old building and says, "This is a famous museum in Paris."

I answer, "What is the Louvre?" which nets me an additional $2,000, but I'm still in a pitiful position to head into the Final Jeopardy! round.

At the end of the Double Jeopardy! round, Samantha has $8,400, Jacob has $7,200 and I have a measly $4,600. Winning now will be nearly impossible.

I give the shark's tooth in my pocket a quick squeeze, because I feel my one and only opportunity to win on *Jeopardy!* slipping away. Maybe Dad was right when he told me all those years ago that I wouldn't do well on this show. I look at Jacob and Samantha. Their backs are straight. They are smiling. They belong here. They deserve this.

But do I?

Alex announces the category for the Final Jeopardy! round and something inside me shrivels.

That's it. I'm sunk.

What Is Olivia Bean Really Good At?

I bite my fingernail while I think, even though Maggie said not to do that.

I imagine Tucker and the big map on his bedroom wall. I remember the hours and days he spent quizzing me with flash cards and atlases and websites. I think of the questions he asked me again and again.

You can do this, Bean.

But then I think of Dad. His voice is like a drill in my mind. *Geography just isn't your thing.*

I feel anger rise inside me.

Dad's not here now, is he? Maybe I *am* good at geography.

My fingers turn to icicles around the stylus—the electronic pen we use to write our responses.

How much should I wager? Nothing. I'm not good at

geography. But I might be, after all of Tucker's help. Tucker wouldn't have spent all that time tutoring me if he didn't believe I could do it.

Suddenly, I hear Tucker's voice in my head. But instead of saying "Olivia Bean, Hula Hoop Queen," he's saying "Olivia Bean, Geography Queen." And even though I might not be able to answer the question, I listen to Tucker's voice and bet everything I have. I write $4,600 with the stylus pen and squeeze the shark's tooth one last time. I don't want to let Tucker down. Or my family.

I take a deep breath and can't believe it when the Final Jeopardy! clue is revealed. I'm so glad I bet the farm on it, as Dad would say.

Jacob must have thought he needed to worry only about beating Samantha, because he wagered $1,300. He must have realized that if she got it wrong, that was all he needed to beat her score.

Even though Jacob gets the answer right, he ends up with only $8,500.

Samantha gets it wrong. *She gets it wrong!* She writes, "What is Rome?"

But I don't. I write the correct answer, thanks to Tucker. And I bet everything and end with a total of $9,200.

That means I, Olivia Bean, Trivia Queen, WIN!

But I don't win $9,200. I win $15,000 and a cruise to Alaska!

My heart pounds faster and harder than a herd of elephants on a rampage because I won *Jeopardy!*

On a geography question.

Alex Trebek walks over and shakes my hand. "Congratulations, Olivia," he says. "You really pulled that out at the end."

Mom, Neil and Charlie charge onstage, hugging me and patting me on the back and shoulders. Samantha and Jacob congratulate me too, as do their parents, who have also come onstage.

"I did it," I whisper to Mom.

"You did," she says.

Neil raises my hand in the air. "Way to go, Brainy Bean."

Charlie hugs me so hard I lose my balance for a second.

The best part is that right now, I don't even care that Dad's not here to celebrate. Although it would have been great for him to see me win.

On. A. Geography. Question!

Who's Sworn to Secrecy?

Afterward, in the green room with Mom, Neil and Charlie, Dad calls on Mom's cell.

"Hey, Butter Bean," he says.

I cringe.

"Sorry I couldn't make it, baby."

Dad keeps talking—explaining—but I tune him out. I don't pay attention again until he says, "Can you tell me who won?"

I remember Maggie and the producer, Rebecca, both said we must be sworn to secrecy until the show airs—two months from now!—about whether we win or lose.

"I can't tell you," I say. "They don't let us." But really, I don't want to tell Dad. If he had been in the audience, like Mom and Neil and Charlie, he'd know that I won. We're only allowed to talk about this with family and the other contestants. It was Dad's choice not to be here. He could have seen me play if he had really wanted to.

"Come on, Jelly Bean," Dad says. "I'm your father. Besides, I can bet some guys on the outcome and make a pile of money. And that would be a very good thing for your dad right now."

I press my lips together and say nothing.

"I'll share some with you," he says. "With your mother."

Heat explodes across my cheeks, but I keep my lips pressed tight.

"Come on, Butter Bean."

I shake my head, not believing what I'm hearing. But really, I do believe Dad would bet on the game . . . because *that's who Dad is*. I decide to take a page from Dad's playbook and say, "Um, Dad. They need me on the show. I've got to go."

"But Olivia, I—"

I hang up and hand the phone to Mom.

She looks at me and tilts her head.

I take a deep breath and say, "Hey, Mom, mind if I make a call?"

"Of course." She hands the phone back. "It's your day, Livi."

I think about it—getting on *Jeopardy!* *and* winning, being surrounded by the people who love me and having fifteen new red umbrella friends. (even if the alternate isn't going to get a chance to play, she is still pretty cool.)

It *is* my day.

Even though a part of me finally understands that Dad is never going to be the father I wish he would be, I still feel pretty terrific.

I dial Tucker's number and hunch forward, fingering the shark's tooth in my pocket.

"Bean!" Tucker says, like he couldn't be more happy to hear from me. "How's it going? You beat those other doofuses yet?"

It's so great to hear his voice. My heart speeds up. "It's over," I say.

"Really?" he says. "Did you win?"

"I can't tell you."

"What?"

"Sorry." I bite a fingernail. "I'm only allowed to talk about it with immediate family and the other contestants."

"That's okay, Bean," Tucker says. "I know you won because you're smarter than any of those other kids."

I'm glowing. "Thanks," I say. "But, Tucker, there's something I think it's okay to tell you. And you won't believe it!"

"Hit me," he says, and it reminds me of Dad not being able to talk to me on the phone because he was at the blackjack table in Las Vegas.

I push that thought out of my mind. "The Final Jeopardy! clue."

"Yeah?" Tucker says. "What was it?"

I picture him leaning forward, the phone pressed against his ear.

I whisper, "The final question was about geography."

"Oh," he says. "How'd you do? Great, right?"

I love that he's so confident in me. "Tucker," I say quietly, "the answer was: *This is the place where democracy began.*"

"No way!" Tucker screams in my ear.

"Yes," I say, nodding so hard I give myself a headache.

"My grandma, who's a geography nut, asks me that one like every time I visit her," Tucker says. "That's why I asked you, Bean."

"Well, thanks," I say, thinking of all the hours Tucker spent helping me, even though I wasn't always nice to him. "I couldn't have done it without you . . . and your grandmother."

"You're welcome, Bean."

"And Tucker . . ." I want to tell him I understand why he called me Olivia Bean, Hula Hoop Queen. I want to tell him I realize he was being nice, not mean. But I just say, "Thanks for all your help."

"That's okay, Bean," he says. "You can pay me back by going to Friendly's with me when you get home. To celebrate, I'm going to get a sundae with *five* scoops of ice cream and *five* toppings . . . and you're treating!"

"Okay," I say, giggling. "That's a deal."

"And by the way, DJ's doing great. I already checked on him twice today, gave him plenty of water and scratched behind his ears."

"Thanks for taking care of Double Jeopardy, Tucker."

"No prob, Bean."

After I hang up, Neil asks, "Everything okay?"

"Definitely."

"Well, Livi," Mom says, looping her arm around my waist. "When this show airs, we'll have a big party."

"We will?" Charlie asks. "Can I invite my teacher, Ms. Bailey-Rioux, and my whole class except for Jeanne Epstein because she sat on my lunch on purpose once, and can we invite Hammy, the class hamster, and—"

"Yes," Mom says. "We're going to invite everyone, even the woman who delivers our mail."

For some reason, this makes us all laugh.

But I know the only people I care about coming to the party are Mom, Neil, Charlie and Tucker. And maybe Tucker's grandma.

Maggie comes into the green room. "It's time to go

back to your seats in the audience," she says. Then she winks at me. "Congratulations, Olivia."

"Thanks."

As we walk down the hallway together, I'm grateful to watch the other kids play, knowing I'm done.

Mom holds my hand as we walk.

"Mom?"

"Yes, Livi?"

I stop walking. "Do you think you could, I don't know, write to Nikki or call her or something?"

Mom tilts her head.

"I think it would mean a lot to her. I think she really misses you."

"Sure." Mom shrugs. "Why not? I always liked Nikki. I'll get in touch with her as soon as we get home."

"Okay." I squeeze Mom's hand to say thanks, and we keep walking.

Charlie, holding Neil's hand, says, "Did you know the average human being makes twenty-five thousand quarts of spit in a lifetime, enough to fill two swimming pools?"

"You don't say?" Mom pretends to throw up.

"Cool," Neil says. "Keep those, ahem, interesting facts coming, little man."

"I will." Charlie grins.

And I grin too.

WHAT IS *JEOPARDY!* TRIVIA?

1. Merv Griffin created *Jeopardy!* in 1963, and it first aired in 1964.

2. Merv Griffin came up with the idea on a flight to New York with his wife, Julann. She suggested giving answers instead of questions.

3. The "Think Music" in the background was originally created by Merv Griffin as a lullaby for his son.

4. Alex Trebek began hosting the show in 1984.

5. Before that, Art Fleming was the popular host.

6. The show's announcer, Johnny Gilbert, also began in 1984.

7. Two hundred thirty *Jeopardy!* shows are produced every year. Each show contains 61 Jeopardy!, Double Jeopardy! and Final Jeopardy! "answers." That's 14,030 answers per year!

8. To learn more about becoming a contestant on Kids Week, check out this link:
jeopardy.com/beacontestant/contestantsearches/

About the Author

Growing up in Philadelphia, Donna Gephart loved fascinating facts, ghoulish ghost stories, corny comic books, perplexing puzzles, and her purple banana-seat bike, which she often rode to the Northeast Regional Library. She still loves riding her bike to the library and reading all kinds of stories, but now she lives in South Florida with her family and writes books for kids. *How to Survive Middle School* garnered starred reviews from *School Library Journal* and *Kirkus Reviews*. *As If Being 12¾ Isn't Bad Enough, My Mother Is Running for President!* won the prestigious Sid Fleischman Humor Award. Visit Donna on the Web at donnagephart.com.